GREAT IRISH SPORTS STARS

SHAY GIVEN

NATASHA MAC A'BHÁIRD is a freelance writer and editor. Her first two children's books, *Missing Ellen* and *Olanna's Big Day,* were both chosen for the White Ravens Collection. She is the author of eleven books for children, including the *Star Club* series, *My Ireland Activity* series, *Reindeer Down* and *Great Irish Sports Stars: Sonia O'Sullivan.*

Natasha didn't play many sports as a child, but has now found an outlet for running around through parkrun. She also loves supporting the Donegal GAA and Republic of Ireland soccer teams and her daughters' teams.

GREAT IRISH SPORTS STARS

SHAY GIVEN

Natasha Mac a'Bháird

THE O'BRIEN PRESS
DUBLIN

Dedication

To Aidan, my favourite person to talk football with.

First published 2021 by
The O'Brien Press Ltd,
12 Terenure Road East, Rathgar,
Dublin 6, Ireland
D06 HD27
Tel: +353 1 4923333; Fax: +353 1 4922777
E-mail: books@obrien.ie
Website: www.obrien.ie
The O'Brien Press is a member of Publishing Ireland.

ISBN: 978-1-78849-258-4

Cover design by Emma Byrne
Internal design by Emma Byrne
Cover illustration by Eoin Coveney

A donation has been made to the Irish Cancer Society.

8 7 6 5 4 3 2 1
23 22 21

Printed and bound in Great Britain by Clays Ltd, Elcograf S.p.A.
The paper in this book is produced using pulp from managed forests.

CONTENTS

PROLOGUE

The night before the match, Shay had trouble sleeping. He was suffering from jet lag due to the time difference between home and Tehran, and nerves didn't help. He couldn't stop thinking about how much they had to play for. He'd missed out on the chance to play at the World Cup four years earlier. Now he was absolutely desperate to make his World Cup dream a reality.

As they made their way from the team bus into the stadium, the players were pelted with fruit and tomatoes by the hostile Iranian fans. The attempt to intimidate the visiting team was starting before they even made it into the stadium.

Shay couldn't believe that there were thousands of fans in the stands already. There were still five hours to go until kick-off! They were shouting abuse at the Irish players, trying to make them feel threatened, overawed by what they had to face. As the goalkeepers went through their stretches, the fans started throwing bangers at them. The noise made them jump! The team were glad to get back to the dressing room to regroup before the match began.

Coming out onto the pitch was like entering a cauldron. The stadium was completely full now and the noise was incredible. Shay couldn't remember ever having played in such an intimidating atmosphere. The small group of Irish fans down one end were proudly displaying their flags and chanting 'Olé, olé, olé', but they were easily drowned out by the home support.

It had been eight long years since Ireland qualified for the World Cup. Shay had watched the USA 94 World Cup on television as a young fan and dreamed of one day representing his country on the world stage. He knew that, back home in Ireland, millions of fans would be tuning in right now, hoping and praying to see their country make it to Japan and Korea.

With the two-goal cushion from the first leg, the

main priority for Ireland was to stop Iran from scoring. The pressure was on the goalie and his defenders to keep that ball out of the net. Iran needed to score two goals to make things level, but Shay was determined not to let them score at all.

'Come on, lads!' he roared. 'Keep things tight!'

Shay made some great saves. In the second half, Ali Daei's shot looked certain to go in, but Shay punched it away just in time.

The ball fell to Karim Bagheri, who immediately took another shot. Shay dived to save it once more, scrambling it out for a corner.

It was a pivotal moment in the game. Shay felt that if that ball had gone in it would have been impossible for the Irish team to stop Iran from scoring for another thirty minutes. The triumphalism of the Iranian fans would make the atmosphere even more unbearable, and it would be so easy for the fight to go out of the Irish.

Minavand was free on the inside left and sent a beautiful half-volley towards the goal. Shay leapt up to his right to knock the ball away. He was having a torrid time of it with so many attempts on goal. He knew he had to stay at the top of his game to keep them from scoring.

The ninety minutes were nearly up. The scoreboard read 0-0. But there was still a minute to go, and then injury time, and the players needed to see this one out.

Goal! Golmohammadi had put the ball in the back of the net, and there was nothing Shay could do about it.

Still a minute of injury time to go. Just hang on, just hang on, Shay said to himself, desperately willing the time to go by. If they didn't concede again, Ireland would be through, 2-1 on aggregate.

Ireland took the kick-off to restart the match. Gary Breen passed the ball back to Shay. Shay's heart was in his mouth as he rushed out to clear it before an Iranian player could try to take advantage. He watched in relief as the ball sailed high and far up the pitch.

The final whistle went. Ireland had done it! Shay and the rest of the team hugged each other in delight, hardly able to believe it.

They were going to the World Cup!

CHAPTER ONE

FOOTBALL CRAZY

There was never a dull moment in the Given house.

Shay shared a bedroom with his three brothers. There were two double beds in the room – one for Marcus and Kieran, and the other for Liam and Shay.

One side of the room was nice and peaceful. Marcus was very laidback, and Kieran wasn't one to pick a fight either, so their bed was a calm place.

The other side of the room was a different story. Shay and Liam both had hot tempers and the slightest thing would set them off, pushing and shoving each other.

'You're not to cross this line,' Liam told Shay,

drawing an imaginary line down the middle of the bed. 'This is my side. Stay on your own.'

'Fine with me!' Shay said, turning over on his side with a thump and taking most of the duvet with him.

But in the middle of the night, a stray foot or elbow would creep over Liam's line, and a scrap would break out once again. On the bedroom door, Shay had stuck up a poster of Ireland and Juventus footballer Liam Brady. The caption read 'Thanks to football for showing me the world.' Shay would gaze at the poster and think how great it would be to see the world thanks to football.

Shay loved having three brothers to play football with. Their big front garden made the perfect GAA or soccer pitch.

'Come on, lads. Three and in! Shay, you're in goal first,' Liam said.

Three and in was a game where one of the boys would go in goal while the other three all tried to score goals against him. Whoever got to three goals first would then take over as goalkeeper.

'I'm always in goal,' Shay complained, but he didn't really mind. He enjoyed playing in goal, always on the lookout for where the threat was coming from, always ready to react.

Shay loved to commentate on the matches at the same time as playing. He'd pretend to be his hero, Everton goalkeeper Neville Southall.

'Another brilliant save by Neville Southall,' he roared as he stopped Liam from scoring with a perfectly timed dive.

On the hill overlooking the house was St Patrick's Church, with a peaceful graveyard beside it, and that was where Mum lay. It was a comfort knowing she was so close. Shay could feel her presence looking down on them and minding them.

Shay was just four years old when Mum died. He was the fifth of six children. Liam, his oldest brother, was eleven, then came Kieran, Marcus, Michelle and Shay, and lastly Sinead, who was two.

Shay had only a few memories of that terrible time. In his mind's eye, he could see Mum sitting up in her hospital bed, her black hair flowing around her thin shoulders. She was smiling at her children, telling them to look after each other.

They celebrated Christmas early that year, in the strange surrounds of the waiting room at the hospital. The younger children didn't really understand, but they were excited by the presents. Kind-faced nurses came and went, whispering to each other, putting on bright cheerful voices for the children, comforting Dad.

Shay knew, because Dad told him later, that Mum made him promise to keep all the family together. 'Hold them together, Seamus,' she'd said. 'You're to hold them together.'

Dad's sisters, wanting to help out, had offered to take a child each to live with them, but Dad had firmly refused. 'They're my children, and they're staying here with me,' he said, and that was the end of it.

The devastating loss of Mum was a tragedy they would all have to learn to live with – but they would do it together.

Dad ran his own market garden business. The fields

around the Given house were planted with potatoes, carrots, turnips, lettuce and beans. It was all hands on deck when the vegetables needed to be harvested.

Weeding was a job Shay hated. The market garden right beside the house was like a window display for everything that Dad's business sold, and it needed to look perfect if it was to attract customers. Keeping it clear of weeds was Shay's job, and it was a slow and thankless task. Up in the big fields they could use ploughs to keep weeds under control, but here in the market garden it had to be done completely by hand because of the small space.

Then there was the job of selling the vegetables, driving round in the van to make deliveries. When they were teenagers, Shay and Marcus often did this job after school or at the weekend.

Dad worked very hard, and he expected all the children to work hard too. When lunch was ready, Michelle or Sinead would blow on Dad's referee whistle, and they'd all come charging in to devour a huge pile of sandwiches. They barely had time to finish eating before Dad would be ordering them back to work.

But there was plenty of time for fun too. Dad played for a football team and he'd bring the children along to watch him on a Saturday afternoon. Sometimes they brought a ball and had their own kickabout while the match was on. But as he got older, Shay was more focused on watching Dad. He was a brilliant goalkeeper and Shay loved to watch him play.

The best spot to watch a match was near the halfway line, so you could see all the ebb and flow of the game. But Shay never stood there. He stood behind the goals, watching every move Dad made, learning from him.

Shay played himself too, both soccer and Gaelic. He preferred soccer, but he knew the skills he was picking up in Gaelic, catching and kicking the ball, would stand to him in the future as a goalie.

When he grew up, he wanted to be a top-class keeper, just like Dad.

CHAPTER TWO

FAMILY LIFE

Every morning at 7am, the key turned in the back door and Mrs Kerrigan let herself in. She was the housekeeper, who looked after the children and did the cooking, cleaning and washing that seemed never-ending in a home with six children.

She'd get them all ready for school, make their lunches and keep the home running while Dad was busy working.

She stayed until 7pm when Dad arrived home, exhausted after a busy day at work, in time to put the children to bed.

They all loved Mrs Kerrigan, who couldn't do enough for the family.

When Mrs Kerrigan's husband fell ill, she had to leave to take care of him. The children missed her very much – her warm, kind presence in the home had been so reassuring after their mother died.

Several different housekeepers and babysitters followed, a string of new faces in the busy household, helping to keep things ticking over as Dad worked hard on his gardening business.

Liam was the oldest, and he was mad about The Smiths. One of their singles had a picture of Elvis Presley on the front, with his hair in a perfect quiff.

Liam got it into his head that he wanted to look like Elvis. He bought some hair dye in the chemist and sneaked off to the bathroom when the house was quiet.

Shay, Kieran and Marcus were kicking a football around in the front garden, and Shay wondered where Liam was.

'Go and find him,' Kieran said. 'We need him to play a proper game.'

Shay ran into the house, checking the kitchen,

sitting room and the boys' shared bedroom, but there was no sign of his eldest brother.

Shay walked into the bathroom and stopped dead. There was Liam, his curly blond hair now pitch black!

'Oh my God,' Shay said. 'Dad's going to go nuts!'

Liam was starting to have second thoughts. 'Is it that bad?' he asked, turning this way and that to examine his head in the mirror.

Shay just burst out laughing, then quickly dodged out of the way as Liam tried to grab him, running straight back out to the garden.

Kieran and Marcus demanded to know what was going on, but all Shay would say was, 'Wait and see!'

At teatime, Liam appeared with a cap on his head. Dad sat down in his usual place at the head of the table. They were all tucking in to the tasty meal prepared by the latest housekeeper when Dad noticed Liam's cap.

'Take that cap off, Liam,' he said. 'It's bad manners wearing that to the table.'

Liam said nothing, just staring at his plate and eating as fast as he could.

'Did you hear me, Liam?' Dad said sharply. 'I said

take that cap off.'

Liam stood up. 'It's all right, Dad, I'm finished eating now anyway.'

He headed straight for the stairs, but Dad was right out after him and yanked the cap off his head.

'What the hell have you done?' he roared. 'Your lovely hair!'

Dad stormed back into the kitchen. 'There's something wrong with your brother,' he told the rest of the children. 'The state of him!'

Shay didn't dare to look at his brothers or sisters. He knew if they caught each other's eyes, they'd all end up in fits of laughter.

Some years after Mum's death, Dad fell in love again. He brought Margaret home to meet the children.

Six faces stared up at her from the kitchen table.

'What a lovely family!' Margaret said. 'Aren't you the lucky man, Seamus? Now, who's who?'

Margaret soon became a part of the family. When she and Dad got married, she left her own home to move into theirs. Two new siblings, Jacqueline and

Paul, came along to join the family, which was then busier and noisier than ever!

Shay loved being part of this hardworking, busy family. There was always something going on, someone to play with or fight with, and the sound of laughter ringing out was never far away.

CHAPTER THREE

BOYS IN GREEN

For as long as he could remember Shay and his brothers had supported the Republic of Ireland soccer team. They'd had brilliant trips to Dublin to watch them play at Lansdowne Road. It was a long drive to Dublin from Donegal but that didn't cost them a thought. Dad would load them all into the car and off they'd go, bouncing around in the back seat, punching each other, arguing about what to put on the radio, thrilled to be missing school to watch the boys in green.

On one trip, Dad insisted that they had to leave earlier than usual. Margaret waved them off, glad that for once the house would be a little bit more peaceful with some of the noisiest members of the family gone for the day!

When they got to the outskirts of Dublin, he didn't head towards the city centre as usual, but turned off towards the airport.

'Where are we going, Dad?' Liam wanted to know. 'This isn't the way to Lansdowne Road.'

'You'll see,' Dad said.

He parked in the car park at the airport hotel. By now the boys were nearly bursting with curiosity. Dad switched off the engine and turned around in his seat to grin at them all.

'What's going on?' Kieran demanded.

'How would you like to meet the team?' Dad asked.

'Are you serious?' asked Shay.

'I've arranged it all with Packie,' Dad said.

Packie Bonner, the Ireland goalkeeper, was a real hero to all the Given boys, and indeed to fans all over the country. He was one of the big stars of the team who played at Euro 88, the first time Ireland had qualified for a major tournament.

What was even more special for them was that Packie came from Donegal. For Shay in particular, seeing a Donegal man playing in goal for his country was amazing. Every time Packie was named in the starting eleven for an Ireland match, he felt they were in safe hands.

Dad knew Packie from football circles, and he had arranged with him for the boys to meet the team.

They couldn't believe it. Shay scrambled out of the car and Dad had to stop him from running straight into the hotel.

In the lobby, Packie came out to meet Dad, and they chatted. More of the Irish players appeared, including Paul McGrath, and they stopped to chat to the Given boys and sign their autograph books. Shay was totally starstruck, finding it hard to believe he was really meeting his heroes.

'Well, what did you think?' Dad asked as they left.

'Brilliant,' said Shay.

'Amazing,' said Liam.

Dad grinned. 'Right, we'd better get going, see if we can make it to Lansdowne before the team bus!'

When Ireland qualified for the World Cup in 1990

the boys were so excited. Shay couldn't wait to watch his heroes play at Italia 90.

Big Jack Charlton had already led his team to the finals of Euro 88, the first time Ireland had qualified for the European Championship. Now they wanted to show what they could do on the world stage.

As the World Cup drew near it seemed like the whole of Ireland was going a little bit mad with excitement. The streets were decorated with Ireland flags and bunting. World Cup songs were being played everywhere. At school, the children talked non-stop about the next match.

'We're all part of Jackie's army,' went the chorus of the most popular song, 'Put 'Em Under Pressure', and it could be heard day and night throughout Shay's house.

When the matches were on, the country came to a standstill, with everyone glued to their TVs. The Given house was just the same. After a game, Shay and his brothers would be straight out to the garden to try to recreate the goals they'd just seen.

'Kevin Sheedy shoots – he scores! Sheedy puts the ball in the England net!'

But of course, when they recreated the games,

Ireland always won.

'Lineker takes a shot, but Packie has him covered! The big man from Donegal saves!'

Shay dived full length, picturing himself stopping England's top striker from scoring.

He loved watching all the team play, but especially Packie Bonner. He'd keep a close eye on Packie's positioning, when he came rushing out for crosses and when he hung back, guarding his goal. He noticed how he got the ball back to his teammates, sometimes having to make a quick decision to release the ball under pressure, and sometimes taking his time to choose the perfect pass.

Big occasions like World Cup matches were always celebrated with Football Special. This was a fizzy drink made by McDaid's in Ramelton and could only be found in Donegal. When you poured it into a glass, it developed a frothy head that made it look like a glass of beer!

After three draws in the three group games, Ireland had made it through to the knockout stages. They would play Romania for a place in the quarter-final.

The countdown to the match was on. The football games in the garden grew even more frenzied as Shay and his brothers imagined how the match might go.

'Niall Quinn scores to win the match for Ireland … Packie Bonner pulls off another wonder save …'

The whole family crowded around the TV to watch the game. After ninety minutes and then extra time, the teams were still scoreless, so it all came down to a penalty shootout.

'Come on, Packie!' Shay shouted. 'You can do it!'

Shay remembered Packie's stunning performance against England at Euro 88, when he made no fewer than twenty-three saves to ensure Ireland's 1-0 victory after Ray Houghton's goal. Could he be the hero again today?

Tension was high as the players took their penalties. After four each, the score stood at 4-4.

Packie Bonner took his place between the goalposts once more, his jaw clenched, a look of grim determination on his face. Shay felt like he was right there with him. He knew just how he must feel.

Romanian player Daniel Timofte took the penalty – and Bonner saved! As he jumped in the air with sheer joy, the Irish fans in the stands went crazy.

At home, the roof was nearly lifted off Shay's house with the roars from all the family. Ireland were one penalty away from the quarter-finals.

As Dave O'Leary stepped forward to take the fifth penalty, commentator George Hamilton said the words that would go down in sporting history: 'A nation holds its breath.' O'Leary calmly slotted the ball into the back of the net.

They had done it! Shay bounced around the room in delight, watching the rest of the team rush to Dave O'Leary to celebrate with him.

'Come on! We need to celebrate this in style!' Dad said.

They all piled into the car and drove into Lifford, car horn blaring, windows rolled down, the children shouting to their friends and neighbours. It was bumper to bumper through the village with so many people doing the same thing. People spilled out of pubs where they'd been watching the match to wave and shout at the passing cars. Children ran up and down carrying Ireland flags and singing songs.

Ireland were through to the quarter-final of the World Cup, and the happiness was so real you could see it everywhere you looked.

For the quarter-final, Ireland were drawn against the host nation, Italy. They could hardly have come up against tougher opposition! But the country continued to dream – until Toto Schillaci broke Irish hearts with his first-half goal. Try as they might, the Irish players couldn't find an equaliser. The match ended 1-0. Ireland were out.

It was a heartbreaking end to an incredible tournament for the boys in green. Shay knew he'd never forget the special memories they had created – and especially Packie's famous penalty save.

'I want to play for Ireland someday, Dad,' he told him.

'You will!' Dad told him. 'You'll play for Ireland before your twentieth birthday. Just you wait and see.'

Dad's rock-solid belief in him gave Shay so much confidence.

CHAPTER FOUR

LIFFORD CELTIC

That summer Shay attended a training day with Packie Bonner, organised for local kids with a keen interest in soccer. He was so excited to meet his hero again and see him in action.

Packie showed the kids some moves and put them through some football drills. Shay relished the chance to watch what Packie did and learn from him.

At the end of the session, Packie signed autographs for everyone. Shay went home clutching his with pride. He really hoped he'd be following in Packie's footsteps one day.

By now football was Shay's whole life. Lifford Celtic were his team. He played for them all through the underage levels.

He was fifteen when the team manager, Robbie White, rang Dad to talk to him.

'I want to put Shay into the men's team,' he said. 'Do you think he's ready for it?'

'Of course he is,' said Dad at once.

'I know he's still only fifteen,' Robbie said.

'He's good enough, so that means he's old enough,' Dad said.

He told Shay the news. 'That was Robbie White on the phone, Shay. He wants you to play for the first eleven.' The pride was clear in Dad's voice.

'Are you serious?' Shay asked.

'Of course,' Dad said. 'You're wanted for the match on Saturday, so have those boots shined and those gloves ready!'

Shay couldn't believe it. What an honour, to be asked to play for the men's team at just fifteen!

He was full of nerves lining out for his first senior match, but the older players soon made him feel at home. They refused to let the opposition bully their young goalkeeper – they were straight in to defend him if anyone was trying to intimidate him.

Growing in confidence, Shay quickly learned how

to organise his defence. From his years of watching Dad, he knew how important it was for the goalkeeper to tell the players in front of him what to do. The goalie could see the flow of the game and be alert to any dangers. Shay had no problem roaring at the back four to tell them where to go and who to mark.

'Paul, look out for the number nine! Jimmy, watch your right shoulder! Mind the gap, Mike!'

The more he talked to the defenders, pointing out threats that they might not have seen, the less likely it was that he'd have to try to make a save. The irony was that some of the best work done by the goalkeeper couldn't be seen by a casual spectator, because it meant that the ball came nowhere near him.

Playing in goal took a lot of courage. Shay needed to be brave in coming out to win crosses, pushing past strikers who were bigger and stronger than him. He had to decide when to come out of his goal to win a ball ahead of an attacker, and when to hang back and play it safe.

It also needed intense focus. Other players might be able to get away with switching off for a few minutes, but not the goalie. A moment's distraction could be enough to give away a goal.

As well as being the last line of defence, the goalie was the first line of attack. With a powerful throw timed just right, or a perfectly placed long kick, Shay could start a movement that led to a goal for Lifford Celtic. It was a thrill to be able to influence the game in such different ways.

Lifford Celtic were an amateur team, but there was nothing amateur about their attitude. The players all took the game very seriously, and Shay learned so much from playing with them.

CHAPTER FIVE

ST COLUMBA'S

Shay didn't enjoy school. He just wasn't a fan of sitting at a desk and learning – he preferred to be out and about, keeping active, playing sport and meeting people. He felt much more at home out on a pitch where his real strengths lay.

He played every sport the school offered – soccer, Gaelic, basketball and volleyball. He even tried rugby for a while but gave it up after getting a whack in the nose!

He loved when one of the school teams had a match and he got to miss class to head off on a bus with his teammates for whatever challenge lay ahead.

Sometimes, too, he missed whole days of school

because Dad needed his help with the market garden business.

'You only come to school when there's a match on!' one of his teachers told him. 'You're missing out on an education and you'll regret it someday. If you think you can make a career out of sport you're in for a disappointment!'

Shay was determined to prove her wrong. Plenty of people did make a career out of sport, and he was sure he had the talent to do it. He just needed to keep working hard at training and doing his best.

St Columba's College soccer team had qualified for the All-Ireland U-14 final. Shay scored a wonder goal for the team, which everyone was talking about afterwards.

'Shay, that was a brilliant goal,' Mr Rodgers, the coach, said. 'I think you've got a great future as a forward.'

Shay loved playing as striker. That year, he was the top scorer for the U-14 team. Scoring goals was always a thrill. Seeing the ball hit the back of the net, wheeling away to celebrate with his teammates, hearing the roar of the spectators – it was hard to beat that amazing feeling.

Playing in goal, as he did for Lifford Celtic, was a tougher job. People were quick to blame the goalie when things went wrong, and even when you'd had a really good game you didn't always get the credit you deserved.

Sometimes Shay found himself torn between the two roles. But when he thought of the future, of making a career for himself in football, he could see himself following in Dad's footsteps and being the one to stop goals rather than score them.

St Columba's already had a brilliant goalkeeper, Peadar. He had been singled out by Packie Bonner at a training workshop as a goalie with great potential, and he was first choice for the school team. So for a long time Shay got to play both roles – goalie for Lifford Celtic, striker for St Columba's. Gabriel played up front alongside him on the school team, and they made a brilliant pair.

'Great goal, Shay!' Gabriel roared, rushing over to clap him on the back.

'Brilliant assist, thanks!' Shay told him. 'I couldn't miss from there!'

Then one day, Mr Rodgers came to talk to Shay.

'Peadar's injured,' he told him. 'I know you're a

great keeper. Can you play in goal for the match tomorrow?'

'No problem, coach!' Shay said. He was happy to step in when the team needed him.

He caught up with Peadar later. 'Sorry to hear you're injured,' he said.

'I hate having to miss the match,' Peadar said gloomily. 'Don't get too comfortable there in goal, will you?!'

Shay felt bad for Peadar, and he couldn't help wondering too if he'd find it frustrating being stuck in goal if the team were struggling to score. But at the same time, it was exciting to have the chance to show what he could do for his school as an experienced keeper.

CHAPTER SIX

ALL-IRELAND FINAL

By the time Peadar was fit to play again, Shay was firmly established as the first-choice keeper for St Columba's. Now it was Peadar who was his understudy. Playing in goal felt like a natural fit to Shay. He sometimes missed the thrill of scoring goals, but he knew the team were relying on him to run things from the back and that was a great feeling too.

The school had qualified for the U-18 All-Ireland Final. They'd be up against Greenhills from Dublin. Shay was still only fifteen, but he was as good as any of the seventeen-year-olds on the team, if not better.

The day of the final came. It was to be played in

Finn Park in Ballybofey, the home ground of the biggest soccer team in Donegal, Finn Harps. Shay and his teammates were determined to show these Dublin boys just how well football was played in Donegal!

As the two teams lined out, Shay eyed the opposition nervously. They were big lads, two or three years older than him, and Shay was still fairly small for his age. Could he really do what was needed to stop them from scoring? Suddenly he felt his sense of confidence fading away. This was going to be really tough.

At last the match was underway. Shay barely had time to register what was happening before the attacking team were closing in on him. BOOM! The ball was in the back of the net!

Shay couldn't believe it. The game was less than a minute old and already he had conceded a goal. He felt as if all eyes were on him as he went to get the ball.

'Wake up, Shay!' Johnny told him. 'You can't be letting in goals like that!'

Shay said nothing. He knew Johnny was right. He kicked the ball towards the centre circle for the restart and went back to his line, not looking at anyone.

The game got underway once more. Shay was relieved to see Gabriel winning a long ball at the far end of the pitch. Gabriel took a shot, but the ball went wide.

Before long the Greenhills players had the ball in the St Columba's half of the pitch. A tall, well-built boy was bearing in on goal when Fergal put in a sliding tackle and took him out.

The referee blew his whistle for a foul.

'Ah, come on, ref!' shouted Shay and his teammates. But the referee was having none of it. Greenhills had a free kick, in a deadly spot just thirty metres out from goal.

Shay roared to his defenders to form a wall. The boys were still lining up when the Greenhills forward took the free, trying to catch them off-guard. The ball went around the wall, but it was a weak shot that just trickled along the ground.

Shay came out to collect the ball, wanting to get it out of the danger area as quickly as he could. Somehow – he had no idea how – he fluffed this simple task and the ball slipped between his legs.

The crowd roared. The ball was in the back of the net!

Shay put his head in his hands. What a disaster! Two goals down after just a few minutes!

A minute later, trying to quickly pass the ball to Fergal, Shay instead put it right in the path of an oncoming striker. He watched horrorstruck as the Greenhills player took a shot. The ball went to the left and wide. Shay heaved a sigh of relief.

'Come on!' he told himself fiercely. 'You can do better than this!'

But he never got the chance.

The game was just nine minutes old when Shay saw Mr Rodgers signalling from the sideline that he wanted to make a substitution. Shay wondered if Fergal had hurt himself in that sliding tackle minutes earlier, but Fergal turned to Shay.

'It's you he's calling. You're off,' he told him.

Sure enough, there was Peadar on the sideline, pulling on his goalie gloves.

Shay stared at him in horror. He knew he wasn't playing well, but there wasn't even ten minutes gone in the game. Surely Mr Rodgers would let him play on and give him a chance to redeem himself.

Peadar was jogging slowly towards him, head down, not happy at being put in this position. Shay realised that this time everyone really was looking at him. He trudged off the pitch, wishing the ground would open up and swallow him.

'Not your day, son,' Mr Rodgers said, patting Shay on the shoulder. Shay shrugged him off. He didn't want sympathy. He felt utterly humiliated at being taken off so early.

The rest of the match went by in a blur. Greenhills College were completely in control, scoring goal after goal. St Columba's managed to get two back, but when the final whistle blew the scoreline stood at 7-2 to the Greenhills boys.

When Shay saw Dad afterwards he was furious. 'What the hell was that coach thinking, taking you off so early?' he fumed. 'You'd barely had time to get into your stride! Who does he think he is, humiliating a young fella like that? I've a good mind to go and tell him exactly what I think of him.'

'Leave it, Dad,' Shay said. It was a comfort knowing that Dad was on his side, but he didn't want a fuss.

'He needs to cop on!' Dad ranted. 'That's no way

to treat his players. And it's not like Peadar did any better, letting in another five! Well, he'll have to manage without you next time, so he will.'

'What do you mean, Dad?' Shay asked in alarm.

'I'm not letting you play for him again,' Dad said. 'I won't have him treating you like that. That's not on.'

'Don't say that, Dad,' Shay said. 'I don't care about what happened today – I want to play again next week.'

'Well, we'll have to see about that,' Dad said, storming off towards the car.

St Columba's were due to play in the U-16 final the following weekend. All week in school the talk was of the awful goal Shay had conceded and how terrible it was to see him taken off.

'Forget about it, Shay,' Peadar told him. 'They were a good side! I couldn't stop them either.'

But Shay found it hard to stop thinking about the match.

All week, too, Dad threatened that he wouldn't

let Shay play for St Columba's again. Dad had a hot temper and was often issuing threats, but Shay worried that he really meant it. Despite the humiliation of being taken off so early against Greenhills, all he wanted was to get out on the pitch again and show what he could do.

Mr Gleeson did his best to lift Shay's spirits. 'Don't worry about it, Shay,' he said. 'We all have bad days. We know what you can do. You'll be starting in the final on Saturday, so put it behind you now and look forward to that.'

Mr Rodgers, too, tried to reassure Shay. 'I'm sorry I had to take you off,' he told him. 'But I could see your confidence was gone. I thought I was doing you a favour, to be honest.'

By Friday evening Dad still hadn't said it was OK for Shay to play in the final. Shay knew the coaches wanted him there, and he wanted to be there more than anyone.

'Dad, you have to let me play,' he urged. 'I want to prove I can do it! It'll look really bad if I just walk away from the team.'

'All right so,' Dad said gruffly. 'But you just remember you're better than any of them. You go out there and play a blinder, you hear me?'

'I will,' Shay said, grinning.

And he did. His confidence restored, Shay played a fantastic game. Just minutes into the match, the ball was heading straight for the top corner before Shay pulled off a brilliant save.

'Well done, Shay,' the coaches roared.

It was a tight game, but St Columba's won by the narrowest of margins, Alan Oliver scoring the winning goal. When the final whistle blew Shay ran towards the centre circle to celebrate with his teammates. They'd done it! St Columba's were All-Ireland U-16 Champions!

CHAPTER SEVEN

FAI JUNIOR CUP

Shay was fifteen when Lifford Celtic made it to the quarter-final of the FAI Junior Cup in 1992. The word junior meant that it was a competition for amateur teams, not that it was for underage teams. In a nationwide competition with 400 clubs taking part, it was a brilliant achievement for a small club from Donegal to make it to the last eight in Ireland, and the whole town was buzzing.

They were to play Bagenalstown FC in the quarter-finals, and Shay couldn't wait.

With just a few weeks to go before the match, Shay was playing in a basketball match for St Columba's. He leapt to stop a shot and fell awkwardly. When he looked down at his wrist, it was twisted out of shape. The pain was horrendous.

An X-ray confirmed what Shay was afraid of. His wrist was broken.

'But Dad, what about the quarter-final?' Shay said, almost in tears.

Dad looked at the doctor, who shook his head. 'There'll be no sport for a few weeks, son. We need to get that wrist in plaster and give it time to heal.'

It was agony to have to miss the most important match Lifford Celtic had played in. But they made it through, which gave Shay a month to get his wrist healed for the semi-final.

They were due to play Neilstown Rangers at Oriel Park in Dundalk. Shay desperately wanted to play. Every day he flexed his hand, trying to see if his wrist felt like it was getting stronger.

At last the day came to get the cast off.

'How soon can he get back playing?' Dad asked.

Shay was on tenterhooks waiting for the answer.

'As soon as you like,' the doctor said. 'That bone has healed well, and you're young and healthy, so off you go. I hope I won't be seeing you back here any time soon!'

It was the news Shay had been longing to hear

– and so had Dad. As soon as they got home he picked up the phone and started making calls.

Dad had been involved in Irish football for decades, and he had contacts from far and wide. He had an important message for scouts.

'Get yourself to Dundalk on Saturday,' he said. 'There's a young lad playing in nets for Lifford Celtic and you don't want to miss him.'

CHAPTER EIGHT

SHAY IN THE SPOTLIGHT

It wasn't the match Shay had been hoping for. Neilstown were a tough team. Just before half-time, Shay conceded a goal, and that was it. Lifford played their best, but they couldn't get back into it.

But that was far from the end of the story.

Dad's phone calls had paid off, and several scouts turned up to see Shay. In the days that followed, offers of trials to play in England started to roll in.

'Bradford City want you over,' Dad told Shay. 'Now's your chance to show them what you can do.'

Shay was very excited. The Bradford City manager was Frank Stapleton, a legend in Irish football. Shay had grown up watching him play, and remembered his heroics at Euro 88, when he was captain of the Irish side. He had scored twenty goals for Ireland and been a star player for both Man United and Arsenal.

Shay got a flight from Belfast by himself and he was picked up at the airport and taken on a tour of Valley Parade, the Bradford stadium. The next day, he flew with the team to Germany for an under-19s tournament.

It was all very new and exciting for a fifteen-year-old from a small town. But Shay wasn't fazed by the football – by now he was well used to playing with men years older than himself, so a team still in their teens was no bother to him.

He enjoyed the trip and played well, but he wasn't in a rush to sign for Bradford. Frank Stapleton tried to convince him it was the way to go – learning the game and working his way up. But by then, bigger clubs were interested in Shay.

'I've had a call from Liam Brady,' Dad told him. 'Celtic want to have a look at you too.'

'No way,' Shay said, thrilled.

Growing up in Donegal, following Celtic was a big part of Shay's life. The Glasgow team had so many links to Ireland, and their goalie was none other than Italia 90 legend Packie Bonner.

Now Celtic were coming to Dublin for a pre-season tour. Liam Brady, the team manager, rang Dad to invite Shay to come and meet the team.

Liam Brady was another Irish football hero, one of the most skilled midfielders to ever play for Ireland. He'd played for Arsenal and Juventus and won seventy-two caps for the Republic of Ireland. Shay thought of the poster he'd had on his bed-room door of Liam in the black and white stripes of Juventus. To hear that he had personally phoned up to invite Shay on a trip to Dublin was unbelievable.

The squad were staying in the Burlington Hotel, and Shay went to join them. Checking in to the hotel with Dad, Shay tried to take it all in. He was staying in the same hotel as the Celtic first team, and he'd be joining in their pre-season preparations, just like another member of the team. For a whole week he would be training, eating and hanging out with some of his heroes, like Packie Bonner and Gordon Marshall. Shay tried to play it cool, but it was hard to hide how excited he was to be there.

From the start the other players made Shay feel

like one of the gang. Sitting around the table in the grand hotel, chatting and laughing over lunch, they made sure to include him in their conversations, asking him about the team he played for and his ambitions in the game. Shay was thrilled to be involved with them all.

The team went to the training grounds at University College Dublin for a session. Shay saw straight away that this was going to be a tough one. Liam Brady had set it up so that there were twice as many attackers as defenders, and the goalkeeper had to work non-stop to keep the ball out of the net. First Gordon Marshall went in goal, then Packie Bonner – and then it was Shay's turn.

'You need to be good here,' Dad told him.

'I know!' Shay said. He didn't need Dad to tell him what a big moment this was.

The pressure was on. Shay knew this was his chance to show what he could do. He concentrated fiercely on the task at hand. He knew he couldn't keep every shot out against players of this calibre, but when his turn was up he felt he'd done well.

It seemed Liam Brady thought so too. That evening, back at the hotel, he took Dad to one side.

'Mr Given, I think we have a star goalkeeper of the future on our hands here,' he told him.

Shay went home to Donegal with a shiny new pair of football boots, gloves and a Celtic training kit, his heart full of hope for the future.

Celtic were keen to sign Shay as soon as possible. But before Shay could make a final decision, Dad got another important phone call.

It was Manchester United manager Alex Ferguson, and he wanted to have a look at Shay.

'Oh my God,' said Shay when he heard the news. 'Man United! But what about Celtic, Dad? Will they be annoyed if I go for a trial with United?'

'No harm in going for a trial,' Dad said. 'You can't pass up an opportunity like this. Celtic will understand.'

So Shay was on the next flight to Manchester.

He was taken straight to United's first-team training ground. It felt surreal to see players stroll past him, men he was so used to watching on TV. He was glued to the spot when he saw Peter Schmeichel, the legendary Danish goalkeeper, and Shay's idol for the last few years.

Dad's words of advice were ringing in Shay's ears as he joined in with training. 'Do your best, work hard, you'll be fine.' It meant a lot coming from such an experienced goalkeeper as Dad.

Shay enjoyed hanging out with the other boys who were there on trial. Like him, they were all dreaming of the chance to make it at a top club.

As one of the biggest clubs in England, Man United had scouts everywhere. They regularly brought in promising young footballers from all over Britain and Ireland, and even further afield, to see if they had what it took to become a professional footballer. Shay was full of hope that he would be one of the chosen few.

They played a game against the United youth team, and the standard was very high. Shay felt sure he'd be seeing some of those players making it all the way in years to come.

Alex Ferguson was very good to Shay, checking in with him regularly. He came up to chat to him in the canteen, wanting to make sure he was enjoying his trial and getting the most out of it.

But Shay suffered an injury in the first week and wasn't able to show United what he could really do. It felt like a major chance had slipped by.

'Don't worry about it,' Alex said in a phone call to Dad. 'We'll look after him.'

After the few weeks were up, Shay flew home, knowing he had a lot to think about. Man United were keen to sign him, but so too were Celtic. Once again, Dad proved to be a great source of advice.

'I think Celtic is the place for you,' he said. 'Let's face it, Schmeichel is going to be first-choice keeper for United for a long, long time. You don't want to head to a big club just to play for the reserves. At Celtic you'll be straight in to the first team.'

Shay laughed. 'I'm sixteen, Dad! I don't think anyone's going to be putting me into their first team.'

'Well, close enough,' Dad said. 'You'll certainly move up the ranks faster at Celtic than you would at United. And you'll have Liam Brady looking out for you, and Packie Bonner too.'

The decision was made. It was off to Glasgow and a fresh new start for the young goalkeeper with so much potential.

CHAPTER NINE

CELTIC

When Dad told the school that Shay would be leaving, the principal tried his best to change his mind.

'He's only just sixteen,' he said. 'Would you not let him stay until he's done his Leaving Cert? He needs to have something to fall back on if football doesn't work out for him.'

But Dad shook his head. 'We'd be mad to pass up a chance like this. And you know yourself Shay's never been much of a student.'

Shay agreed with Dad. Even if football didn't work out, he couldn't see himself studying or wanting a job where he needed to pass exams. He'd come home and work for Dad's business, as he had done all through his childhood.

But he was determined that football WOULD work out. He'd been given a wonderful opportunity by Celtic, and he was going to make the most of it.

The whole family were proud of Shay – it was so exciting knowing he was off to Celtic, the club they'd all followed over the years.

Margaret helped him to pack, making sure he had plenty of clean clothes.

'The house won't be the same without you,' she sighed, folding a pair of tracksuit bottoms and adding them to the ever-growing pile.

Sinead, the sister next in age to Shay, watched with envy. 'I wish I was going away on a trip!'

'It won't all be fun and games,' Margaret reminded her. 'Shay's going to be working very hard. Now, where did I put those socks?'

Dad drove Shay to Belfast and they got the ferry across to Scotland. At Parkhead, Celtic's grounds, a member of the Celtic youth team set-up met them and shook hands with them both.

'You're very welcome, Shay,' he said. 'We hope you'll be very happy here at Celtic. He's in good hands here, Mr Given.'

It was time for Dad to go. Shay could tell he was doing his best to put on a brave face, but he was very emotional.

'Best of luck, son,' he said, turning to get back into the car.

Shay watched the car drive away. He could see Dad's shoulders heaving as he tried to suppress the tears. It only really hit him then that Dad was leaving and he was all on his own in a foreign country.

And so began a strange new life for Shay. He trained every day at Celtic, and went home every evening to where he was staying in 'digs'. This meant that he was living with a family who provided his meals, did his laundry and generally kept an eye on him.

He was well looked after, but he was very lonely. He missed his family, his friends and his own bed. He was used to the hustle and bustle of life in a large family, with all his brothers and sisters. Theirs was a noisy, busy house, full of love and laughter, people coming and going, neighbours calling in. And he was part of a small, close-knit community – if he wandered down the main street in Lifford he wouldn't go more than a few metres without bumping into someone he knew.

Now he was out in the world on his own at sixteen years old. Glasgow felt huge and scary and strange. It would be nearly three months until he could go home for a visit.

Being an apprentice at Celtic was hard work. The young lads would have to clean the first team's football boots and run errands for them. They swept the mud out of the dressing rooms and tidied up. When it snowed, they'd get out the brushes and sweep the place clean.

Shay didn't mind any of it. He knew that the first team had done the same thing when they were apprentices. They'd had to work their way up to the top, and he looked forward to the day when he'd be one of them.

Shay could hardly believe he was sharing a dressing room with Packie Bonner, the hero of Italia 90. It was just two years since he'd watched him make that famous penalty save. Now here he was training alongside him and learning directly from him, one Donegal goalkeeper to another.

Packie was great for passing on tips.

'You need to step off and then dive,' Packie told him. 'That way you build momentum.'

Shay relished the chance to learn from the best. The best piece of advice Packie gave him was that he would always have to keep working hard – there was no such thing as making it to the top and then kicking back and relaxing. Staying on top was even tougher than getting there in the first place and it demanded hard work every day.

Packie kept an eye on Shay, and when he saw the homesickness was getting on top of him he rang Dad and told him to come over for a visit.

It really lifted Shay's spirits to spend the weekend with Dad and Margaret. They took Shay out for a meal and they all went out on a big walk together. Shay told them all about his training and they chatted and laughed about everything that was going on with the family at home.

But all too soon Sunday night came, and Shay was on his own once again.

After a few months the homesickness became overwhelming. Shay rang his brother Liam, who was working in Belfast.

'I can't take much more of this,' he told him. 'I

just want to go home.'

'Stick it out,' Liam advised him. 'It'll all be worth it in the end. Think of how much you dreamed of a chance like this when you were a kid. You'll never be able to live with yourself if you give up now.'

Shay knew he was right, but it didn't make him feel any better. It didn't help that the part of Glasgow Shay was living in was quite rough, and he didn't feel safe being out and about on his own. Eventually he went to speak to Liam Brady about it.

'Leave it with me,' Liam said.

Shay was moved to new digs outside the city centre, along with a lad from Derry. It was like having a little bit of home back, and slowly he began to settle in.

Shay had never had his own money before. Working for Dad, he'd never had a regular wage – Dad would give him a fiver here and there which he spent as soon as he got it. Now he was earning a regular salary, and although it wasn't much, it felt like a fortune to a young lad from Donegal. He saved up and at the end of his first year at Celtic he bought his own car. It was a tiny little two-door

Vauxhall Nova, but Shay felt like he was driving a Ferrari. That summer he took it home to Donegal on the ferry. He was as proud as punch giving his friends lifts and taking them here, there and everywhere.

After two years at Parkhead, Shay's apprenticeship at Celtic was coming to an end. Liam Brady had been replaced as manager by Lou Macari. Shay hoped that he would still feature in the new manager's plans and that the club would make an offer to sign him. But when the offer came, it was disappointing. Shay would be earning less money than he had as an apprentice!

He called Dad to talk it over with him.

'Don't even think about signing that deal,' Dad said. 'You've spent two years away from home, working hard and learning your trade. That's an insult to make you an offer like that. You'd be better off coming home and playing in the League of Ireland.'

Shay knew Dad was right, though he wasn't

keen on the idea of going home. It felt like failure. Dozens of young Irish lads went to the UK every year for trials at football clubs, a smaller number were offered an apprenticeship as he had been, but only a tiny number were offered deals. But Shay still felt sure that the right offer would come, even if it took a little bit longer. His dream was still very much alive.

'Something else will come up,' Dad said. 'You'll get another offer, don't worry.'

So Shay packed his bags and headed for the ferry, his head held high.

CHAPTER TEN

BLACKBURN

Shay didn't have to wait too long for the phone to ring. The Blackburn Rovers goal-keeping coach, Terry Gennoe, had seen him play in an under-19 tournament in Holland, and he liked what he saw.

'Blackburn want us to come and meet them in Dublin,' Dad told Shay. 'I knew you'd get another offer before you were much older.'

The same week, Celtic got back in touch. Once again they had had a change of manager, with Tommy Burns taking over from Lou Macari, and Dad felt they might offer Shay better terms.

It felt good knowing two teams were interested in him. Shay and Dad headed off to Dublin to meet

Kenny Dalglish, the Blackburn manager and an icon in British football.

Dad remembered Kenny Dalglish as a world-class player for Liverpool, Celtic and his native Scotland. Shay could remember the later stages of his playing career, when he'd been a brilliant player-manager for Liverpool, winning league titles, FA Cups and European Cups. To both of them it was a huge honour to meet this inspiring man and know that he was interested in Shay.

Shay got a great first impression from Kenny, who was so encouraging and told him he could learn and develop as a player in the Blackburn set up. He offered him a four-year deal on £500 a week.

To the young Shay, this was an absolute fortune. He couldn't believe they were offering him this kind of money, and he was more than happy to agree. But out of respect for Celtic, he didn't sign anything right away.

Dad spoke to Celtic on his behalf, but after a long discussion they couldn't offer him a deal as good as the one he was getting from Blackburn. So the decision was made.

Shay was sorry to be leaving the club he had supported all his life, but he knew Blackburn offered him the best chance to advance his career. He couldn't wait to get started in the Premier League.

Shay was eighteen now – still very young, but a bit more used to living away from home. He shared a house with two other Irish footballers who were just starting out on their careers in England.

At Blackburn, Shay soon realised he was going to have a hard time getting picked for the team, with two experienced goalkeepers ahead of him. But he relished the opportunities he got in training. One thing that was different about Blackburn was that the goalkeeping coach worked with them full time. It made all the difference having Terry Gennoe coaching him in all the skills – corner drills, free kicks, penalties, and all the different scenarios that might crop up in a match.

Shay loved it. He wished he could train twelve hours a day! He just couldn't get enough.

He had always been very quick in terms of his footwork, and that was something they worked on together to improve further. They also focused a lot on his ability to spring up to catch the ball, high and fast – a skill that would stay with him throughout his career.

Kenny Dalglish was a brilliant manager, and Shay was thrilled to be able to work with him. He knew it was a fantastic opportunity for any young player. Kenny had been a superb player in his day, and even now when he joined in the five-a-sides you could see the depth of his skills. He was a warm, friendly character, always laughing and joking with the players. He made them want to go out and play their hearts out for him – he was able to get the best out of every player.

'Don't get carried away when you're playing well, Shay,' he told him one day. 'And don't get down when you have a bad game, either. You'll have good days and bad days in this game – you have to stay level-headed to deal with both.'

It was a piece of advice that Shay would remember all his life.

The time had come for Shay to go out on loan so he could get some first-team football. Going out on loan was common among young players. It meant the player was still under contract with their original club, but they would play for the new club for an agreed time. It gave them experience and an idea of what first-team football would be like.

Swindon Town were keen to sign him. They were two divisions below Blackburn so it meant quite a drop, but that didn't matter to Shay. The important thing was that they were promising him game time, as their regular keeper was out injured.

Some young players were content to sit at big clubs and not play but that wasn't Shay's style at all. He'd much prefer to be out playing for a lower ranked club like Swindon, developing his skills under the pressure of real matches, than warming the bench at Blackburn.

So Shay's league debut was in a Swindon shirt against Hull City, which meant a six-hour bus drive. It might not have had the glamour of a Premier League tie against Man United or Liverpool, but it meant the world to Shay. At last he could say his football career had really begun.

His first taste of professional football made him hungry for more. He played five matches for Swindon and conceded just one goal before he was recalled by Blackburn.

He didn't stay too long at Ewood Park, because Sunderland asked if he would go there on loan.

'You can have him on one condition,' Dalglish told them. 'He plays.'

Sunderland promised that Shay would get plenty of game time, and they were as good as their word. He joined up with the club and was straight into his first match, where he kept a clean sheet – stopping the other team from scoring any goals. It was the first of twelve clean sheets he would keep over the course of seventeen matches, and he was soon a firm favourite with the Sunderland fans.

Something else happened during his time at Sunderland that would change Shay's life. He caught the eye of Mick McCarthy, the new manager of the Republic of Ireland senior team.

CHAPTER ELEVEN

IRELAND'S CALL

And then came the call Shay had dreamt of all his life. In March 1996 he was called up to play for the Republic of Ireland senior team.

At just nineteen, Shay found himself training with the heroes he'd worshipped from afar – Paul McGrath, Andy Townsend, Niall Quinn and John Aldridge. He'd watched these talented footballers go out and play for Ireland at Italia 90 and USA 94 – and now he was one of them.

It was the start of a new era for Irish football. The hugely popular manager Jack Charlton, who had led the Irish team to their first three major tournaments, had just left. He had been replaced by Mick McCarthy, another Italia 90 legend who had earned himself the nickname 'Captain Fantastic'. He was now making a career for himself in management and for the last few years he had been manager of Millwall.

Packie Bonner had been replaced by Alan Kelly as first-choice keeper for Ireland, and Shay knew he'd have a battle on his hands to take his place. He'd done well when he'd played for the Irish youth teams, but this was a huge step up, and he was still a teenager.

In Mick McCarthy's first match in charge, Ireland were due to play Russia, and the team were training the day before the match when Alan suffered a relapse of a back injury.

Mick showed his faith in Shay. 'You'll be starting tomorrow,' he told him. 'So make sure you have a good night's sleep!'

Shay remembered Dad saying that he'd play for Ireland before he turned twenty. He'd just squeezed in on time!

It seemed that most of Lifford were in the crowd to watch Shay's debut. Dad, Margaret, his brothers and sisters, his aunts and uncles and cousins, his old teammates at Lifford Celtic – they'd all got the bus down from Donegal to be part of Shay's big moment.

The proudest of all was Dad. He had encouraged Shay to believe in his dreams from when he was just a little boy, had given him advice and support at every stage of his career, and had always believed in him.

'Go out there and enjoy it,' Dad said. 'Don't be looking up at the crowd, just concentrate on what you have to do.'

Shay tried to remember Dad's words as he joined the rest of the team in the dressing room. The enormity of the occasion was almost overwhelming. He'd come so far, from his days playing football with his brothers in the front garden, to Lifford Celtic, to Glasgow Celtic, and now here he was about to represent his country.

He thought, too, of Mum and how much she would have loved to be there for his debut. He had no doubt she was looking down on him and minding him as he took on his biggest challenge yet.

In his glove bag Shay had a little bottle of holy water that Dad had given him. It came from St Patrick's Church where Mum was buried, and it was a special link to her and to home. It gave Shay a sense of calm even in this most pressured of situations.

At last it was time to go out and warm up. Shay was always relieved to get out and get moving. Waiting was the worst part! He felt his nerves start to ease as he warmed up and started diving to save the balls his teammates were firing at him.

Fans were starting to trickle into the stadium. Shay shaded his eyes with his hand as he scanned the stands, hoping to spot a familiar face.

Back in the dressing room, as the team made their final preparations, Shay took his jersey off the peg and marvelled once again. Number one! What an honour and a privilege it was to put that jersey on and go out and represent his country.

'Enjoy every minute, Shay!' Mick McCarthy told him. 'You'll never forget your first match for your country.'

The noise of the crowd hit him as soon as he walked out onto the pitch. The famous Lansdowne Road roar felt even louder from the pitch than it had done when he was just another face in the crowd. The atmosphere was electric. As the national anthem was played, Shay felt his heart would burst with pride.

The referee blew the whistle. Straight away Shay was at work, roaring at his back four to get into the positions he wanted, making sure they were covering all angles. He might be only nineteen and playing for the first time but he wasn't a bit afraid to tell these legends of the game like Paul McGrath where he wanted them. Mick McCarthy trusted him to do his job, and that was exactly what he was going to do.

The senior players made him feel like one of the team from the start.

'You're doing just fine, Shay,' Niall Quinn told him.

It meant a lot coming from one of Ireland's top scorers.

But the team struggled throughout the match, and matters came to a head when Roy Keane was sent off for kicking one of the Russian players. Now they were down to ten men, and the pressure on the teenage goalkeeper was even more intense.

In the end, Ireland lost the game 2-0. It was a disappointing result, but Shay didn't feel too bad. He knew he wasn't at fault for the goals, and he was happy that he'd done his best.

The start of Mick McCarthy's reign was a difficult time for the Irish team. The Italia 90 generation of players were getting older now and they were gradually being eased out of the squad. Now it was up to young players to step up to the mark. It was a particular challenge for their young goalkeeper, having to marshall the defence from the back as they adapted to a new style of play. In a series of friendly matches, they struggled badly, and it wasn't until his eighth game in charge that McCarthy got his first win.

Shay played in the matches against Portugal and the Netherlands, but after that Alan Kelly was back from injury.

'I'm going to play Alan for this one,' Mick McCarthy told him. 'You're not getting enough first-team football at Blackburn, Shay. I need my goalkeeper to be match fit.'

Shay couldn't blame him. He knew how important it was to be getting regular games. He was doing all the training necessary to stay fit and strong, but being match fit was different. It meant having a level of alertness, of quick reaction times, that only came with playing every week.

Although the competition was fierce between them for the number one spot, Shay got on really well with Alan Kelly and also with Dean Kiely, who was battling to be Ireland's goalkeeper too. Shay had always found there was a special bond between goalkeepers – it was the loneliest job on the field, the one where it was so easy to get the blame when things went wrong, and much harder to get the credit for a good performance. The three of them worked together well in training, helping each other to improve, all wanting the best for their country.

For the qualifying campaign for the 1998 World Cup, Shay found himself in and out of the goal-keeping slot. Sometimes Mick would give him the job, other times it would be Alan in goal.

The campaign got off to a flying start with two wins against Liechtenstein and Macedonia and a draw at home to Iceland. But the team couldn't keep up the momentum, and a second place finish in the group meant they found themselves facing a playoff.

Ireland were drawn against Belgium, with the home match to come first.

On the way to the match on the team bus the lads were singing along to Irish folk songs, guaranteed to get them riled up and ready to go. Shay looked around him in the dressing room and felt good about the game to come.

Denis Irwin scored from a free kick early on in the game, and Shay felt his nerves ease a bit. It was the perfect start in front of their home fans – now if only they could hold on for the win.

But it wasn't to be. Belgian striker Luc Nilis scored a brilliant equaliser, and from that point the battle was really on. It was a tough match, neither team giving an inch. When it finished 1-1 the Irish lads trooped off the pitch, knowing they had a lot of work to do for the second leg.

'We know what we have to do now, lads,' Mick McCarthy told them. 'They've got their away goal, so now we need to go out there and score one of our own.'

Heading into the away match, Shay felt confident

that they had what it took to make it to the World Cup. But just twenty-five minutes into the game, he was picking the ball out of his net. Luis Oliveira had managed to skip past him and fire it home.

No one was more thrilled than Shay when Ray Houghton scored an equaliser. Now it was all to play for once more. If Ireland could score again, they'd be ahead on the away goals rule, and Belgium would need to score two.

There were just twenty minutes to go when Ireland went to take a throw. But the referee overruled his own assistants and signalled a throw for Belgium instead. The Irish defence barely had time to get back into position before the throw was taken. Nilis took advantage of a clever overhead pass and blasted it into the net.

That goal would haunt Shay for a long time. He asked himself again and again – had he been too slow to come off his line? Or should he have stayed on his line for longer? What could he have done to prevent that goal? He played it over and over again in his mind, wishing he could change the outcome.

All too soon the referee blew the final whistle. The Belgian players jumped in the air in delight and rushed to embrace each other as the stadium announcer played 'We Are the Champions' over the tannoy.

Shay watched from his lonely spot in goal. Ireland's World Cup hopes were over. Next summer, they'd be sitting at home watching the tournament on TV instead of travelling to France to show what they could do. He felt tears well up in his eyes.

As he joined his teammates to walk down the pitch to salute the Irish fans, he couldn't hold back the tears any longer. He felt he had let everyone down, most of all himself.

He had longed so much to play for Ireland at the World Cup, and now the chance had passed him by. Would it ever come again?

CHAPTER TWELVE

NEWCASTLE

Shay was so excited to be moving to Newcastle United. The Magpies were a top team, regularly finishing in the top four and getting to play in Europe. They had a first-class stadium and a huge following of devoted fans.

Being a professional footballer meant having to up sticks and move your entire life when you changed clubs. Shay would need to find somewhere new to live and get to know the lively city of Newcastle. He'd be the new boy in town, having to get to know a whole new set of teammates and make friends. This was all very exciting and Shay couldn't wait to get started.

Manager Kenny Dalglish was now in charge of

Newcastle United, and he wanted to bring Shay with him. He promised Shay he would be playing regularly for the side. That was massive news for a young footballer. At twenty-one, not many goalkeepers got to play regularly for their clubs, let alone for such a big club as Newcastle.

With three other top goalkeepers playing for Newcastle, Shay knew he'd have fierce competition for that number one jersey. So he was thrilled when Dalglish told him he'd be starting in the first match of the season.

Shay was nervous heading out for that first match against Sheffield Wednesday, but his teammates made him feel welcome straight away, and so did the Newcastle fans. The roar from the home support as the team walked out of the tunnel at St James' Park was a special moment.

And it was about to get even better. Shay's second game for Newcastle was a Champions League qualifier against Dinamo Zagreb. Shay couldn't believe he was playing in such a high-profile match already, and was grateful for Dalglish's faith in him.

Having played in huge matches for Ireland in front of a packed home crowd, a full house at St

James' Park wasn't as daunting as it might have been. Shay relished the opportunity to play on such a big stage.

Newcastle won the first leg and scraped through the second. Now they were really in the big leagues – they would play Barcelona in the Champions League itself.

Shay had only played five matches for Newcastle, but once again Dalglish put his trust in him. He had told him 'You're coming up here to do something memorable' and he was true to his word.

Barcelona were the clear favourites for the match. They were the kings of European football, with a long list of titles and trophies. Their manager Louis van Gaal told the media before the game that he expected them to win – that everyone did. Newcastle didn't have much experience of playing in Europe. But Shay and his teammates were determined to give them a run for their money.

As he walked out onto the pitch, Shay knew it was a night he would remember for the rest of his life. St James' Park was a sea of black and white, fans decked out in shirts and scarves and hats, flags waved frantically in the air. The noise hit him like a shockwave – it was as if it had a life of its own.

Shay eyed up the opposition. Up until now players like Luis Figo and Rivaldo were only names in his Playstation FIFA game. Now it was his job to stop them scoring.

The TV camera zoomed in on Shay for a close-up shot. The Champions League music filled the stadium. This was it!

As the match got underway, Shay was shouting and roaring at his back four as he always did – but they couldn't hear a thing! The noise of the crowd was so intense that he couldn't be heard even two metres away.

Newcastle got off to a dream start with a goal from Tino Asprilla. 1-0! Northern Ireland star Keith Gillespie was sensational on the wing for Newcastle, winning balls and putting in cross after cross. Another goal from Tino – 2-0! And minutes later he had completed his hat-trick.

Shay was roaring like a madman from the other end of the pitch. 3-0 up against Barcelona! Unbelievable! Now they just had to hold on for the win.

The home crowd were going wild, singing and cheering in delight.

Twenty minutes to go, and Newcastle were still three goals up. They couldn't throw this away. Then Luis Enrique scored for Barcelona, and Luis Figo followed suit. 3-2. Shay gripped his hands into fists. There was no way they were getting past him a third time. No way!

He thought the game would never end. When the referee finally blew his whistle, the overwhelming feeling was relief. He rushed to celebrate with the rest of the team. They saluted their fans, who were still screaming their heads off.

He was twenty-one years old, and his team had just beaten Barcelona in the Champions League. Life didn't get much better than this.

CHAPTER THIRTEEN

FA CUP

Newcastle weren't having a great run in the Premier League. By April they were out of contention for the title, and the club's hopes turned to the FA Cup.

When Shay left Blackburn he was hoping to win trophies, and this now looked like a real possibility as Newcastle had made it to the FA Cup semi-final. They were up against Sheffield United at Old Trafford. The final would be held at Wembley, and it was the ultimate dream to be able to play there.

Shay wasn't sure what to expect, so it was brilliant to walk out of the tunnel and see the opposite stand at Manchester United's home ground transformed into a sea of black and white. The Magpies fans had travelled in huge numbers and were roaring their support for their team.

Alan Kelly was in goal for Sheffield United. It was always a bit strange for Shay to have one of his Ireland teammates playing for the other side, and to be hoping to see the ball put past him!

The match was tense, with not much to choose between the sides. At last Alan Shearer broke the deadlock with a scrappy goal for Newcastle. Shay was thrilled! Now it was up to him to guard his net closely to make sure of the win.

The referee blew the whistle. It was all over. Newcastle were through to the final!

Alan Kelly came over to shake his hand. 'Well played, Shay! Best of luck in the final.'

Shay remembered all those times he'd played football in the garden with his brothers, pretending they were playing in a cup final at Wembley. Now he'd get to experience what it was really like.

It would be a long six weeks to wait for the final. It seemed everyone in Newcastle was excited, and everywhere Shay went people were wishing him luck. It had been many years since Newcastle had won anything. Were they the team who would end the long wait for a trophy?

Shay thought back to all the times he'd watched the FA Cup Final day on TV. It would be an all-day event for himself and his brothers – they'd watch the players leaving their hotels, the buses making their way to Wembley, the analysts making their predictions about how the match would go. It all added to the sense of occasion and by the time the kick-off arrived they'd be completely hyper!

Now, wandering around the pitch before the match, wearing his new suit along with the rest of the team, it was pure magic. Shay knew that there would be millions of people watching from all around the world. The FA Cup was one of the biggest competitions in the world. Would it be Newcastle or Arsenal who came out on top?

In the dressing room Shay tried to stay focused, taking sips of water, putting on his gloves and boots. Kenny Dalglish tried to keep them all relaxed. He'd won two FA Cups as a player at Liverpool so he knew exactly how the team were feeling. There was no need for him to make a rousing speech – these lads knew exactly how big this occasion was.

Arsenal were missing one of their top players,

Dennis Bergkamp, which gave the Newcastle boys a bit of a boost. But they were still the top team of the year – they'd already won the Premier League title and were hoping to do the double.

It was time. The two teams made their way onto the pitch, the sun beating down on them. It was a roasting hot day in London and Shay knew it was going to be one of the toughest tests his team would face.

'This is our chance,' Alan Shearer told the team huddle. 'We're not going home without that cup!'

The game kicked off. Shay couldn't help feeling that Arsenal were showing their superiority already. They were strong all over the pitch, and he had to be on constant alert for shots.

Marc Overmars was bearing down on goal. Alessandro Pistone tried to hold him off, and Shay came out, doing his best to look as intimidating as possible. He spread himself out, trying to put Overmars off, but he toe-poked the ball right between Shay's legs.

A goal down already. As the game restarted, Shay hoped and prayed his teammates would get things level again.

He watched as first Dabizas and then Shearer hit the post. They just couldn't catch a break.

'Keep trying!' Shay roared.

Next thing Shay found his defence split again and Anelka, the talented French forward, had taken a couple of touches. Shay dived for the ball but it just shot past him.

That was it. Newcastle were two goals down and the game was slipping out of their grasp.

All the preparation in the world, all the talent and skill and teamwork, and sometimes all you needed was a little bit of luck.

When the final whistle blew, Shay slumped down where he stood. After all the build-up, all the hope and expectation, it was all over.

Arsenal goalkeeper David Seaman came over to shake his hand. 'Keep your head up,' he told Shay. 'There's plenty of time in your career yet.'

Shay really appreciated his kind words, but nothing could take away from his disappointment.

Shay just wanted to go home, but the team had to go up to collect their runners-up medals. It was a comfort to see the Newcastle fans were still in the stands, cheering them on. Shay felt that it showed the deep loyalty the fans had for their team.

Afterwards, sitting down to a meal together, the atmosphere was one of doom and gloom. The players kept going over the match, trying to figure out what they could have done differently, where it had all gone wrong.

Shay couldn't help thinking about how different it must be for the Arsenal players. How were they celebrating their great victory? He could just imagine the partying and celebrations. If only that had been Newcastle! He would have so loved to be enjoying that amazing feeling with his brilliant teammates, knowing that whatever else happened in their careers they would always have those FA Cup medals – but it just wasn't meant to be.

CHAPTER FOURTEEN

WORLD CUP QUALIFICATION

The Republic of Ireland had another chance to qualify for the World Cup. The 2002 tournament would be held in Japan and South Korea, and the team were determined that this time they would be there.

Shay relished the chance to play in the qualifiers. The campaign was going well for Ireland, with a decent record in home wins and away draws. But in order to finish in the top two they knew they would have to beat one of the best teams in the group – Portugal or the Netherlands.

The Netherlands were one of the top teams in the world at that time. In the away match, the game had ended 2-2, a decent result for the Irish side.

Now it was time to take them on in Lansdowne Road.

In the run-up to the game, Shay faced a lot of questions from the media about a mistake he'd made in a recent match for Newcastle. It was the kind of error every goalkeeper dreads. He'd been going to save a shot against Chelsea when the ball had just slipped out of his grasp. Something like that could really knock a player's confidence, but it helped to know that he had the full backing of Mick McCarthy.

'Of course Shay will be starting for us,' he told the media. 'He's my first-choice keeper, and while he's fit he'll play, simple as that.'

Playing in front of Shay, the four defenders were Steve Staunton, Richard Dunne, Ian Harte and Gary Kelly. They brought a mixture of experience and youth to the side. Steve Staunton had been a rock at the heart of the Irish defence since he made his debut in 1988, when Shay was a twelve-year-old fan cheering on the boys in green. Gary Kelly, too, had gone to the World Cup with Ireland in 1994. The other two were younger, with Ian Harte having played for Ireland for the first time in the same year as Shay, and Richard Dunne making his debut in 2000.

From the moment the match kicked off Shay could tell it was going to be a full-on battle. Roy Keane set the tone of the match with a fierce challenge on Marc Overmars after just thirty seconds. Minutes later, the Netherlands had their first shot on target. Shay was forced to dive to save Mark van Bommel's effort.

'Watch it!' Shay roared at his defenders, not impressed that the Dutch had got so close so soon.

It was an action-packed first half, a real battle between the two sides. Jason McAteer put in a cross that Robbie Keane latched on to, forcing the Dutch goalie into a save. A Dutch defender was booked for tripping Damien Duff. Gary Kelly was booked for a foul on Overmars which gave the Dutch a free kick just outside the box.

Shay shouted instructions to his back four. He was horrified to see the ball shoot across the six-yard line to Van Nistelrooy, but the Dutchman saw the cross too late and mis-kicked it.

The teams trooped in for the halftime break with the tie still scoreless.

The second half got underway. Shay was forced to make several saves in quick succession, from Van Nistlerooy and Overmars. Then came another shot from Overmars, which bounced awkwardly. Gasps from the crowd showed what a dangerous ball it was, but Shay skilfully knocked the ball around the post.

Minutes later, he was gutted to see Gary Kelly get sent off for a second yellow card. They were down to ten men – their job had just got so much harder.

Mick McCarthy had to make the decision to take off a forward, and Robbie Keane was the unlucky one. He was young, but already the team were starting to rely on him for goals. Would someone else step up to the plate?

Steve Finnan was the man Mick brought on to help with defensive duties. Shay watched as Finnan played a brilliant ball into the box. Jason McAteer made a fantastic run and fired the ball into the net.

Ireland were a goal up! But there were still thirty minutes left to play and anything could happen.

Now it seemed like the Netherlands were playing with eleven strikers. Attacks were coming from all angles and it was all Shay could do to keep marshalling his defence to keep that ball out of the danger area.

The final whistle blew. Ireland had won! The crowd went crazy, and so too did the players. They'd beaten one of the top sides and now they were guaranteed a playoff place for the World Cup.

Ireland were drawn against Iran in the playoffs. The team knew right away that it would be a tough task. Iran might not be the strongest team in terms of footballing skills, but it was an intimidating place to travel to. Their massive stadium would be a cauldron of noise, filled with 120,000 loud, passionate fans.

The home game was up first. Shay knew they'd need a fine performance all over the pitch to ensure a good result. In particular, there was a huge responsibility on his shoulders. If Iran were to score an away goal, it would make things so much harder for Ireland.

Ali Karimi was one of Iran's most dangerous players. He was through on goal. He took a second too long to take his shot, and Shay dived at his feet to claim the ball. He had timed his move perfectly. The sighs of relief in the crowd echoed around the stadium.

Ireland were two goals up, thanks to Robbie Keane and Ian Harte. But Shay was still determined not to concede. That lead would be so important going into the second leg.

Ali Karimi was on the ball again. Shay watched and waited, knowing he would soon be needed once more. Karimi took the shot, firing it in low to Shay's left. Shay dived and saved it. Another crucial save!

The match finished 2-0. Ireland had given themselves the perfect start – but there was still the away leg to come.

'It's going to be tough out there,' Mick McCarthy warned his players. 'They're going to make things as difficult for us as they can. Don't be expecting a luxury hotel or gourmet food – it's all going to be rubbish. We're there to do a job, and that's what we'll do.'

The away match against Iran was one of the toughest tests Shay had faced in his career. Mick had warned the team that the huge crowds of hostile fans would make for an intimidating atmosphere, but nothing could have prepared them for the harsh reality of having bangers thrown at them and abuse raining down on them before the match even got underway. It was going to be a long ninety minutes.

Shay vowed to stay focused on his vital role as the last line of defence. They had a two-goal lead going into the match, so it was up to him now to make sure they held on to that lead. He needed to be on high alert to stop Iran from scoring and breaking Irish hearts.

Saving one shot after another, Shay wondered how long they could hold on for. He willed the clock to speed up. All he wanted was for the ninety minutes to be over and Ireland's World Cup place secure.

Conceding a goal right at the end was a blow. But they were still 2-1 up on aggregate, and if they could keep it like that, they'd be going to the World Cup and Iran would be staying at home.

'Come on, come on!' Shay thought to himself.

'Blow the whistle, ref!'

At long last the final whistle came.

Relief and joy flooded through him. It was over! A 1-0 defeat on the day, but that didn't matter. They had done what they needed to do, and the prize was all they had ever dreamed of.

The players rushed to hug each other, beaming from ear to ear.

'We've done it!' roared Jason McAteer. 'We're through!'

'Come on!' said Shay. 'We have to go and thank the fans.'

The small group of Irish fans who'd made the long, difficult journey to Iran were going wild with joy. The team went over to salute them. No doubt many of this devoted crew would be booking their flights to the Far East next summer.

The dressing room was buzzing. Mick McCarthy was going around with a huge grin on his face. He'd played at the World Cup himself in 1990, and now he was going to lead his team there as manager. What an achievement!

'You saved us out there, Shay,' he told his goalkeeper. 'We'd be going nowhere if it wasn't for that performance!'

Shay was so proud to have played his part in getting Ireland to a much longed-for World Cup.

When the team plane took off that night to head back to Dublin, the players, fans and media were all singing songs and celebrating together.

Their World Cup adventure had begun.

CHAPTER FIFTEEN

SAIPAN

May 2002. The World Cup was a few short weeks away, and the Republic of Ireland team travelled to Saipan, a small island off the coast of Japan, to get used to the hot climate and begin their preparations.

Shay was thrilled to be on his way to the World Cup. He remembered all too well the pain of missing out in 1998, watching the matches on television when he would have given anything to be part of it all.

The trip to Saipan took almost a whole day, with three flights. The players were exhausted by the time they arrived at their hotel, a beautiful old building whose grounds stretched right down to the beach.

They had just finished a long, tiring season with their clubs. They were all looking forward to a bit of rest and relaxation before they started gearing up for the tournament.

The Ireland team came from a mixture of different backgrounds and played for clubs like Newcastle, Man United, Man City, Leeds and Aston Villa. They ranged in age from youngsters like Robbie Keane to elder statesmen like Steve Staunton and Niall Quinn. Robbie, the twenty-one-year-old striker from Tallaght, was the life and soul of the party, always up to mischief, playing tricks on his teammates and keen to have a laugh. Damien Duff was a much more laidback character who loved his bed more than anything else. Any time they had a break he'd head back to his room for a nap!

Lee Carsley, on the other hand, would use any spare half hour as a chance to go to the gym. Others preferred to play table tennis, go for a swim or sit around drinking coffee and chatting.

Niall Quinn was a great storyteller. He had a few tall tales up his sleeve, but his reminiscences about Italia 90 and the Jack Charlton era were what the younger players were always eager to hear.

As the old man of the group, Steve Staunton was often horrified at the music the youngsters were listening to. 'Turn off that racket, some of us are trying to sleep!' he'd roar at them. But they knew he was always there for any younger player who needed a listening ear.

Shay loved hanging out with this team, who had come so far together. They were a diverse group, but together they were united behind one goal – getting the best possible results for Ireland on their World Cup journey.

A light training session was planned for their first day in Saipan. But when they arrived at the training ground, everything started to go wrong.

The pitch was in terrible condition – dry and stony and full of potholes.

'It's like a car park,' Roy Keane said in disgust. 'You can't expect us to train on that!'

As well as the state of the pitch, there were more problems. The team's equipment hadn't arrived. They had no cones, no bibs, no energy drinks – and no footballs.

'So what?' Shay said. 'We'll just wear our own gear and do a fitness session, it's no big deal.'

'It's ridiculous,' Roy fumed. 'What a shambles!'

Roy was the team captain. He had always been a hot-headed character, passionate about football, expecting high standards everywhere he went, and with no tolerance for any shortcomings.

'I'm not happy about this at all,' Mick McCarthy told the players. 'This shouldn't have happened. But we'll just have to manage as best we can.'

Most of the players just shrugged their shoulders and got on with it. But Roy wasn't happy. Later, Niall Quinn tried to smooth things over with him.

'Come on, Roy, it's not the end of the world,' he said. 'We're all in this together. Let's just laugh it off and get on with things.'

Roy was having none of it. 'It's wrong, that's all there is to it.'

When the team turned up for their second training session, things went from bad to worse. After the complaints about the pitch being dry, the groundsmen had reacted by flooding the area overnight. This hadn't done much to improve matters. It still left them with a bad playing surface, bobbly and uneven.

Roy's mood turned even blacker. He was looking

for someone to lash out at – and he found his target in the goalkeepers.

Packie Bonner, now the goalkeeping coach for Ireland, had asked Mick if the goalies could start their training session earlier, before the sun got too strong. Training for goalkeepers was intense – they might not run as far as the outfield players, but they were constantly up and down, diving, leaping, recovering their position. It was hard work and it was made even tougher in the searing heat of the eastern sun.

By the time their session was over, Shay was exhausted. It was hard to breathe in the hot, humid conditions, and he was glad to sit down with the other keepers, Alan Kelly and Dean Kiely, in a tent at the side of the pitch, out of the sun. They were gulping down water, trying to cool down after the gruelling session.

Roy Keane came marching over looking for some goalkeepers to take part in a seven-a-side session.

'They're knackered,' Packie told him.

'They're supposed to be knackered, it's a World Cup,' Roy retorted.

Alan Kelly backed up Packie, telling Roy that it was none of his business how the goalkeepers trained.

Roy stormed off. Shay couldn't figure out why he was getting so worked up. He had always been a bit hot-headed during training sessions, screaming at people for bad passes or if he felt they weren't trying hard enough. But this was taking things a bit further. Maybe the pressure of the World Cup was getting to him.

Later that day, a rumour went around the squad that Roy was going home. Colin Healy, who was on standby for the squad in case of injuries or other emergencies, was getting ready to fly out to Japan to replace him.

Shay couldn't believe it. Surely Roy wasn't going to throw away the chance to play in the World Cup? He was their captain – they needed him now more than ever.

It seemed the row had blown over, and Roy was at training again the next day like the rest of them. Afterwards, Shay saw him talking to two of the journalists who had flown out to Saipan to cover the build-up to the World Cup. He didn't think anything of it. It was normal for the players to do media interviews at some point, so he presumed it was Roy's turn today.

He had no idea that Roy had lit a powder keg and it was about to explode.

That evening the players were sitting around the ballroom of the hotel. They'd eaten their fill from the buffet and were enjoying live entertainment from the in-house band.

Mick McCarthy came in carrying a copy of *The Irish Times*. He stood waiting for the band to finish their song, then politely asked them to leave.

Shay sensed that something major was about to happen. The players were on edge as the band shuffled out, waiting for Mick to speak.

Mick went over to Roy Keane and showed him the paper. 'Roy, care to explain this?'

Roy had done an interview with the paper, criticising the preparations for the camp in Saipan, the poor facilities and lack of equipment, and Mick was not a bit impressed.

Roy exploded in a torrent of abuse, telling Mick exactly what he thought of the FAI, the whole team set-up, and Mick himself.

Shay could only sit there in shock. He understood why Roy was unhappy but he felt he had gone too far.

After what felt like an eternity, Roy finally stopped. Mick was still outwardly calm as he said, 'Well, I don't know what happens now. Because either you go or I go. And I'm going nowhere.'

Roy stood up and looked around the room. 'Good luck lads, all the best,' he said. And he walked out.

For a moment there was a stunned silence in the room. The players couldn't even look at each other, staring instead at their feet in their flip-flops, the tablecloth, the fan whirring around on the ceiling. No one knew what to say.

At last Dean Kiely broke the tension. He was the third-choice goalkeeper, a hardworking, decent player. 'Boss,' he said to Mick. 'If you need a midfielder, I can play there – I'll do you a job.'

The squad burst out laughing. It was the perfect way to break the tension. Mick looked around at them all, still shell-shocked.

Gary Kelly turned to him. 'We're with you, Mick,' he reassured him. 'We have to stick together. Now are we behind Mick or not?'

The rest of the players started clapping to show their support. The senior players – Niall Quinn, Steve Staunton and Alan Kelly – promised to sit beside Mick at the press conference that would be held later to explain the bizarre news to the waiting media, to show that he had their backing.

The team were united. They would get through this together.

But the fact remained that Ireland were facing into the World Cup without their captain, their leader on the pitch and off – their best player.

CHAPTER SIXTEEN

WORLD CUP 2002

Shay couldn't get his head around all that had happened. For as long as he could remember it had been his dream to play at the World Cup. Now he was there and it felt like everything was falling apart around him.

Roy was such a key part of the Irish side, organising the team on the pitch, encouraging and berating them, keeping things tight at the back and creating chances up front. There was no doubt that they were a weaker side without their captain.

He understood why Roy was annoyed at everything that had gone wrong with their preparations. But Shay knew that nothing in this world could stop him putting on the jersey and going out to play for Ireland. If he'd had to row to Japan in a canoe he would have done it, because it meant the world to him.

The day after the big row, the team flew to Izumo in Japan – and Roy flew home to Manchester. The deadline had passed to name the final squad, so it was too late for Colin Healy to take his place. Ireland would be one player short. Shay tried to put it all behind him and focus on what lay ahead.

The first group game was against Cameroon. Warming up before the game, Shay kept an eye out for his family. Dad, Liam and Paul were all there to support him, and he knew Liam would have his 'OK SHAY' banner with him. Sure enough, there it was, big and bold. It gave Shay a lift knowing they were so close.

He knew, too, that the rest of the family would be watching on television back home in Lifford. Jacqueline, his seventeen-year-old sister, was doing her Leaving Cert, and Margaret had stayed home to look after her, but they wouldn't miss a moment of the action.

He thought of Mum and how proud she would have been to see her son play in the World Cup. He said a little prayer, as he always did before a game.

In the huddle before kick-off the new captain, Steve Staunton, told his teammates to express themselves and not to be shy. 'Don't anybody hide out there. Remember, no regrets!'

As he stood with the rest of the team to sing the national anthem, Shay felt the hairs stand up on the back of his neck. He could hardly believe he was really here at the World Cup, in a game that would be watched by millions around the world.

Cameroon were a good side, and they proved it by scoring the first goal in the thirty-ninth minute. The Irish players didn't panic. They were confident they would get back into it. Sure enough, Matt Holland scored in the second half to make it 1-1. Shay hoped they could get another goal and take all three points, but the goal never came. A draw was a good start to their campaign – and a good way to put the Saipan affair behind them.

Next up came Germany, one of the greatest teams in world football. Their star striker Miroslav Klose was one to watch, and Shay knew he'd have a busy game.

His opposite number was Oliver Kahn, one of

the best goalkeepers in the world. Shay counted him among his heroes, and it was a thrill to play against him.

A header from Klose gave Germany an early lead. Shay knew that as long as it stayed at 1-0 Ireland had a great chance to get back into the game, and he was determined to keep them from scoring again.

Michael Ballack passed to Carsten Jancker who was clear in the box. Shay rushed out to confront him, putting him off his stride. He sighed in relief as Jancker's shot went wide.

The clock was ticking down, and there was no sign of an Irish goal to level things up. Shay was happy to see Niall Quinn come on. He was tall and imposing and an expert at winning long balls. His height meant he could easily outjump most defenders. Bringing him on always helped to mix things up a bit.

It was up to Shay now to put more long balls in for Quinny. Route One football – bypassing the midfield to hit long balls into the box in the hope that a forward could latch on to them – sometimes got a bad name, but it had worked well for Ireland in the past.

They were into stoppage time now. Last chance saloon. Steve Finnan sent a long ball forward. Quinn leapt in the air and headed it into the path of Robbie Keane. Keane was through on goal with only the keeper to beat. He took his shot and blasted it past Oliver Kahn.

1-1! The Irish fans in the crowd went crazy. Robbie did his trademark cartwheel celebration and the other players hugged him and each other, hardly able to believe it.

All on his own at the other end of the pitch, Shay punched the air in delight as the final whistle blew. What a result!

Afterwards, the Irish physio Mick Byrne went into the German dressing room and asked Oliver Kahn for his shirt for Shay. Shay knew he'd treasure it forever – the perfect memento of a perfect day.

There was just one group game left, and it was against the weakest team in the group, Saudi Arabia. Ireland had a great chance of making it to the knockout stages, and they did it in style, with Robbie Keane, Gary Breen and Damien Duff all putting the ball in the net for a 3-0 win.

Qualifying from their group was a fantastic

achievement for the Irish team. After everything that had happened in Saipan, they felt they had proved all the doubters wrong. Next they would face their toughest task so far – a knockout game against Spain.

The team were hyped up before the match. They knew how much it meant to the people back home, to the fans who had travelled, to their families and friends.

Shay remembered the thrill of watching Italia 90 and seeing Ireland progress to the quarter-final. Wouldn't it be amazing to be part of the team that did that again?

He thought of the children back home in Ireland watching on TV. He imagined them playing football in their gardens and pretending they were at the World Cup, just like he and his brothers had done. He would love to give those young fans something wonderful to celebrate.

From the first whistle Ireland went out fighting. But the wind was knocked out of their sails when

Spain got an early goal. Fernando Morientes scored in the eighth minute.

'Keep the heads up!' Mick shouted. 'Early days!'

Damien Duff might enjoy a snooze any chance he got, but on the pitch there was nobody more alert. He was one of Ireland's star players, weaving in and out between defenders and causing panic with his quick feet. Shay watched from the other end of the pitch as Damien skilfully dribbled the ball into the box and was about to put in a cross when Juanfran made a desperate lunge to stop him. The referee blew his whistle and pointed to the spot. Penalty!

Shay was full of confidence when he saw Ian Harte stepping forward to take the penalty. Harte was the team's dead-ball specialist, who had created many chances from corners and free kicks. There was no way he would miss.

But Harte's shot was nothing like his usual. Shay watched in horror as Casillas made an easy save.

The game was entering its final minutes. They were managing to keep things tight at the back and Spain hadn't looked like scoring again. But neither had Ireland.

In the dying seconds of the game, Steve Finnan put a long ball into the box. Quinn tried to jump for it, but Spanish defender Hierro was holding his shirt.

The referee had a clear view of Hierro's foul and straight away he pointed to the spot. Penalty!

The Spanish players protested wildly, but the referee was adamant.

Ireland had a chance to take the game to extra time.

This time it was Robbie Keane who stepped forward. The young striker had scored a brilliant goal against Germany and was already showing signs that he'd be a force to reckon with for years to come.

Coolly confident, Robbie slotted the penalty home. 1–1!

The final whistle blew. The game was going to extra time. Shay hoped that his teammates could find a goal in the next thirty minutes and save him from the horror of penalties.

But after 120 minutes of football, the sides were still level at a goal apiece. Penalties it was.

Shay and the other goalkeepers had practised saving penalties again and again. It was a psychological challenge as much as a physical one. Could you read the player's intentions? Was he going to hit it to the right or left? High or low? If he had gone to the left the last three times in a row, would he do the same again, or was this the time he'd switch it up? Was it better to take a guess and dive early, or wait until the player had taken his shot?

With a perfectly hit penalty shot, a goalie had no chance. But even the best strikers in the world didn't always take the perfect penalty.

Shay thought back to Packie Bonner's famous save against Romania twelve years earlier. His fellow Donegal man was a hero to this day. Shay wanted more than anything to follow in his footsteps.

As a goalie, he never got to score a match winner. A penalty shootout was a rare chance to be the hero of the hour.

The team gathered around the manager to plan their strategy.

'Just do me one thing,' Mick told them. 'Pick a spot and stick with it. Don't change your mind.'

Shay knew it was good advice. As a keeper, that moment's hesitation, that indecision from a striker made it much easier to stop the shot. He wished he could take a penalty himself! He'd had more dead-ball practice than anybody else and felt he could take one well.

Robbie Keane was first up for Ireland. He put the ball in the back of the net. Hierro stepped forward for Spain and blasted it home. 1-1.

Then things started to go wrong. The next three Irish players – Holland, Connolly and Kilbane – all missed their penalties. For Spain, only Baraja had scored.

Ireland needed to put the fifth penalty away or they were gone. Steve Finnan came up to the spot, and Shay was relieved to see him score.

Now it was all down to him. The score stood at 2-2 and Spain still had a penalty left to take. If he could save it, it would go to sudden death.

Gaizka Mendieta took his time, strolling to the penalty spot as if he was just out for a walk. He carefully positioned the ball the way he wanted it.

Shay tried to stare him down, tried to get inside his head. But Mendieta seemed impossibly calm.

What do I do now? Shay asked himself. Stand firm and wait until he takes his shot, in the hope that it might go down the middle, or might not have enough power on it? Or just pick a side and dive?

I have to go for it, Shay decided. Better to dive the wrong way than to stand there looking at a ball blasting past you.

Mendieta took a big run up but his shot was weak, going straight down the middle. Shay had dived a fraction of a second too soon, and the ball dribbled over his leg and into the back of the net.

It had missed his leg by a millimetre. The tiniest of margins had decided this momentous game.

It was a moment that would haunt Shay for a long time. He couldn't stop playing it over in his mind. If only he had stood his ground a bit longer. It was his chance to be a hero, and it had passed him by.

They were out of the World Cup. The moments that followed went by in a blur. The players who had missed penalties were devastated, but no one was more upset than Shay.

It was such a cruel way for his World Cup dream to end.

CHAPTER SEVENTEEN

EMERGENCY

Newcastle were 2-0 up against West Ham at Upton Park. After a slow start to the season, this looked like it could be a turning point.

There were five minutes left on the clock. Marlon Harewood was through on goal. Shay sized things up and decided to come out and beat him to the ball. When Marlon realised Shay was going to win the ball he tried to draw back, but he wasn't in time. His knees went crashing into Shay's ribcage.

Marlon was a big, well-built player and the collision knocked the wind right out of Shay. He lay on the turf gasping for breath, that horrible, panicked feeling of not being able to get air in.

The medics came rushing on to assess him. Shay

was breathing again, but with just minutes left to play he knew it wasn't worth trying to fight on, so he was relieved to be taken off.

Sitting in the dressing room, waiting for the match to end, Shay didn't feel very well. The team came charging in, delighted with their victory, and asked if he was all right.

'It's nothing serious, I'm grand,' Shay said. But he didn't feel grand.

The team doctor came in to have a look at him.

'I've got this funny feeling in my stomach,' Shay said. 'I can't really describe it.'

'Go and have a shower, and take it slowly,' the doctor advised. 'We'll see how you are then.'

Shay had just turned the water on when suddenly he got a pain so sharp he felt like someone was sticking a knife into him. Waves of burning pain washed over him and he thought he might faint.

He shouted for the doctor, who came rushing in and helped him onto a bed.

'It's OK Shay, you'll be all right,' the doctor tried to reassure him.

But Shay heard nothing more. He had fainted dead away.

When he came to, Shay had been moved to a different room and he was surrounded by doctors. The West Ham team doctor was helping to advise his own team doctor. An ambulance had been sent for.

It was a pain like nothing Shay had ever experienced before. He gripped the sides of his bed, his knuckles turning white, in sheer agony.

At long last they heard the sound of the ambulance siren. The West Ham fans applauded Shay as he was stretchered out to the ambulance. They could see he was in a bad way.

The time that followed was a blur. Shay found out afterwards that he had been diagnosed with a perforated bowel, which was leaking into his system. He was rushed into surgery to repair it. It was a freak injury caused by a collision with the other player, the kind of collision that happened all the time in football and usually led to nothing worse than bruises. The injury he had suffered was more common after a car crash.

The next thing Shay knew, he was waking up in a hospital bed. He had a tube coming out of his nose and he was attached to a drip. He looked down at his stomach and saw that it was covered in bandages.

Shay tried to get his head around what had happened. One minute he was trying to prevent a goal and the next – or so it seemed to him – he was waking up in hospital.

Shay spent the next week in hospital. He had lots of visitors. One of the first people who came to see him was Marlon Harewood, who felt really bad about the injury.

'Don't worry about it, mate,' Shay told him. 'It's not your fault – it was just one of those things!'

Robbie Keane came in with two bags full of chocolate, jellies and cans of fizzy drink.

'Brought you a few treats!' he announced.

'You do realise my stomach is in bits here?' Shay told him, pointing to his bandages.

Robbie could only laugh. It hadn't occurred to him that Shay wouldn't be able for treats just yet. All he could eat was soup!

Shay had messages from lots of different players, especially goalkeepers. Once again they were looking out for one of their own.

It would be a long road to recovery for Shay. He knew he'd need to take things very slowly.

He found it frustrating that he couldn't work on

the injury. It wasn't like a muscle injury where the right physio or stretches could help sort it out. A dip in an ice bath was no good either! He just had to give it time and let nature take its course.

After two months, Shay was able to return to training. His first match was for Ireland. He got a huge welcome from the fans who'd made the trip to San Marino to see their team win 5-0. It felt so good to be back!

CHAPTER EIGHTEEN

MANCHESTER CITY

Shay had been at Newcastle United for twelve years now. He'd committed the best part of his career to the club, and it meant the world to him.

It was hard to imagine leaving Newcastle. He felt so comfortable there – after so many years in the city, he had put down roots, and it was where his children, Shayne and Sienna, had been born. His brother Marcus and sister Sinead lived nearby too, and he had made so many good friends. Moving to a new city at this stage of his life would be very different from when he was younger and only had himself to think about when he was going out on loan or signing for a new club. Now he had settled down and made Newcastle his home.

But things were going wrong at the club. They were in a state of upheaval with managers coming and going at short notice, top players leaving and not being replaced, and a feeling that no one in the club really cared.

The low point came in a match against Liverpool. Shay played his heart out, doing everything he could to keep goals out, and in the first half he managed to keep the opposition to just one goal. But he couldn't do it alone. In the second half, it was like battling against the tide. The final score was 5-1 to Liverpool.

Shay had had enough. He had signed for Newcastle in the hope of winning trophies, and it hadn't happened. He couldn't go on like this, getting battered every week.

He spoke to his agent and they released a statement saying he wanted to leave the club.

Straight away Shay had inquiries from some of the biggest clubs in England. Manchester City, Tottenham Hotspur and Arsenal were all interested in him.

In the end, it was Man City who Shay signed for.

City were a cash-rich club. They could have signed any goalkeeper in the world, so it meant so much to Shay that he was the man they wanted.

The move meant a big change in Shay's life. For the first while, he stayed in an apartment in a hotel, before renting a place of his own.

One thing that was very different was that he was now in a city with two major clubs instead of one. It made it a bit less intense. For the first time in years he could go out and get a coffee without being surrounded by fans.

The training regime at the club was very different. Shay enjoyed the fresh start, and the sense that here was a club with real ambition, where the team were constantly working to improve their game, where he could have realistic hopes of winning titles.

There was strong competition for Shay at Man City. Two goalkeepers were already established there – Joe Hart, the twenty-one-year-old England international, and Kasper Schmeichel, the Danish keeper and son of Shay's hero Peter.

Shay knew he was coming in to be the first-choice keeper, but he also knew he'd have to work hard to keep that role. He had a job to do to prove himself to the manager and staff, to the rest of the team, and to the fans. The Newcastle fans knew him so well, but he was brand new to City. It was up to him to prove to them that he was the right fit for their club.

His debut for City brought a lot of pressure. They were playing Middlesbrough, and Shay was keen to make an impression right from the start.

Having played for one club for so long, it was strange to be the new guy all over again. But Shay had great confidence in his own ability, and he soon had the chance to show what he could do. He made some great saves against Afonso Alves, including one spectacular reaction save from point-blank range. He managed to keep a clean sheet, City winning 1-0 thanks to a goal from another new signing, Craig Bellamy. It made Shay's day to be awarded Man of the Match for his performance.

His Ireland teammate, Richard Dunne, was also at Man City. It was great having a friend at the club, and Shay rated Richard very highly. He was a skilled defender who was never afraid to put his body on the line to stop goals. He was exactly the kind of player Shay liked to have in front of him in the back four.

The three goalkeepers, Shay, Joe and Kasper, trained together. They did regular yoga sessions together too. They were always keen to learn from each other. As the oldest and most experienced player, Shay had more advice to pass on, but he was happy to learn from the younger players too. They were a support to each other – praising each other for good saves in training or matches.

'You had a great game there, Shay,' Kasper would tell him after a match. 'Nice save at the end!'

'Thanks,' Shay said with a laugh. 'I was sure that one was going in!'

Kasper felt that he had a lot to prove because he was following in the footsteps of his famous dad. Shay expected that he wouldn't stay at City for too long because he would be eager to get first-team football. Sure enough, when the chance came to go out on loan Kasper took it.

Joe, too, wasn't happy to just sit on the bench, collecting his wages. He was desperate to get playing.

Shay could see a lot of himself in these younger players. He remembered what it was like to be their age, wanting to get game time and to prove themselves.

Pheeeee! The final whistle blew. Extra time had failed to separate the sides, and now it was going to penalties.

Shay's heart sank. His experience of penalties wasn't good, and he was dreading having to face them again.

It was the second leg of City's UEFA Cup tie against Aalborg. City had won 2-0 at home, but in the last few minutes of the away match Aalborg had got two goals back.

'You can do this,' Shay told himself fiercely. 'This is your chance to be the hero!'

Aalborg had never been involved in a penalty shootout before. Shay hoped this might work in his favour.

He tried to psych them out, taking his time about getting into position, spreading himself out in the goal to look as big as possible, staring them down.

The first two Aalborg players put their balls firmly in the back of the net. But so too did the Man City lads, so it was level.

'This time,' Shay told himself as Thomas Augustinussen ran up to the penalty spot.

Several hundred City fans were behind Shay's goal and were shouting encouragement to him.

Augustinussen looked nervous. Shay tried to stare him down. He took his shot. Shay guessed right – he dived to his right to make an easy save.

City scored. Now they were 3-2 up. Could Shay do it again?

The fourth penalty for Aalborg went in. But Dunne smashed his in too, so City still had the advantage. 4-3. If Shay could save this next shot it would all be over.

Shelton stepped forward. Shay kept the ball in his hands for as long as he could. 'I've got nothing to lose here,' he told himself, trying to stay calm. 'The pressure's all on him.'

Shelton took his shot. Shay dived to the right once more and blocked the shot. He watched it dribble away to safety before he jumped to his feet. The City fans went crazy, and Shay's teammates were all over him. He had done it! City were through to the quarter-final!

CHAPTER NINETEEN

DARK DAYS AT CITY

Sadly that would be as far as they would go in the competition. In the quarter-final City lost 3-1 away to Hamburg. In the return leg, despite a brilliant performance from Elano, they couldn't overcome the deficit and lost 4-3 on aggregate.

It was a sad end to the season, with no trophies to show for all their efforts.

As the new season got underway, City got off to a great start, winning their first five matches – three of them away from home. But it was to be their away form that started to cause problems. One of the low points was a trip across the city to Old Trafford. The lead had swung from one team to the other until Craig Bellamy scored for City in the ninetieth minute to make it 3-3. Shay was relieved that they seemed to have hung on for the draw, but there was no sign of the referee blowing the whistle. Six minutes into added time, Michael Owen blasted the ball past Shay to win the match for United.

The lacklustre draws and disappointing defeats kept coming. Shay tried not to get downhearted – he felt it was still early days, and it would take time to build a winning team. But then manager Mark Hughes was sacked. Here we go again, Shay thought. One of the reasons he'd left Newcastle was the lack of stability with managers coming and going. Now the City bosses were doing the same thing.

The new manager would be the Italian Roberto Mancini, and Shay was worried about what it would mean for his future at the club. Would Mancini want to bring in his own choice of goalkeeper, maybe Italy's top keeper Buffon?

His fears were eased a bit at Mancini's first press conference as City manager, when he described Shay as one of the top five goalkeepers in the world. In the beginning, Shay continued to be the first-choice keeper for City. Results for the club started to improve, and Shay felt that things were looking up.

Towards the end of the season, Man City once again faced their archenemies Man United. Late in the game, Shay dived to try to save a header from Paul Scholes. Landing with a thump, he immediately felt a sharp pain in his shoulder. Even as he watched Scholes running off to celebrate his goal, he knew the injury was pretty serious.

That week, Shay spent a lot of time having physio. Jamie, the Man City physio, told Shay he had strained ligaments in his shoulder and it needed rest.

'I'll be fine,' Shay insisted. 'I can play.'

Any time his team lost, the only thing that made Shay feel better was the determination to get back out there and do better next time.

On the way to the next match away to Arsenal the following weekend, Shay was wincing with the pain in his shoulder. Before the match he had it strapped up, but even in the warm-up he knew he wasn't right.

But he refused to listen to the physios, insisting he was OK to go out and play. Shay had always found that the adrenaline rush of a match would help him play on through the pain barrier.

With twenty minutes left to go in the match,

Shay dived to block a shot from Abou Diaby. Pop! He felt his shoulder pop straight out of its joint.

The pain was excruciating. Shay hadn't felt anything like it since the horrendous stomach injury he'd suffered four years earlier.

The physio confirmed what Shay had feared – his shoulder was fully dislocated. He was stretchered off the pitch. His season was over.

Over the next year, it became clear that Mancini favoured Joe Hart over Shay. Even when Shay's injury had fully healed, Mancini wasn't picking him. Shay still badly wanted to be the first-choice keeper for the club, but he felt that even if he'd got to play in the cup games that would have been something. But match after match, Mancini left him on the bench.

Joe kept on playing well, and Shay supported him as best he could. He didn't blame Joe for the fact that he wasn't getting picked – that was down to the manager and no one else. He didn't enjoy having to play the role of understudy, but he knew it was part and parcel of life as a footballer. Joe had done it for him, and now it was his turn.

May rolled around once more, and City had made it to the FA Cup Final against Stoke. Shay was determined to be as much help to Joe as he could, working hard with him in training, giving him whatever advice he could, offering him moral support.

When Yaya Touré smashed home the winner for Man City, it was an amazing moment. City held on for the win, and when the final whistle blew Shay raced on to the pitch to congratulate Joe. Joe threw his arms around him, screaming in delight, and the two of them leapt around the place, going crazy.

As the team made their way to the celebration stage to pick up the Cup, there was a little ache in the middle of Shay's happiness. It was a strange position to be in. He had an FA Cup winner's medal, but he hadn't played a minute of the final. He was thrilled for his teammates and for all the club's supporters, but he didn't feel the victory was really his.

CHAPTER TWENTY

TRAPATTONI ERA

Whatever was going on with his club, Shay always loved the chance to play for Ireland. A special moment came in a match against Slovakia in 2007. Shay was made captain to mark the occasion of equalling Packie Bonner's record of eighty caps. It was amazing to think he had now played for Ireland as many times as his hero.

2008 marked the start of a new era for the boys in green. The legendary Italian manager, Giovanni Trapattoni, had just been appointed to lead the team, replacing Steve Staunton who had made the move from player to manager without much success.

Trapattoni was one of the most successful managers in world football. He had won league titles in four different European countries, an astonishing achievement, and was one of only two coaches to have won all three major European club competitions.

At first the Irish players found it hard to get to know him as he spoke very little English. But his assistant, Marco Tardelli, had good English and could translate for them. Also part of the management team was Liam Brady, who spoke fluent Italian after his years playing in Serie A. Liam was the one who had brought Shay to Celtic, his first club, so he had a special place in his heart.

Trap was clearly a bit of a character. One of the first rules that he made was that the squad were not to eat mushrooms! Shay couldn't understand it. What was wrong with mushrooms? They often had mushroom soup at the hotel where they stayed when they got together for a home match. But not anymore!

After the bad experience of Staunton's reign, when Ireland had been leaking goals, the priority now was to strengthen the defence. Trap was the perfect manager for this as he specialised in tightening up defences and being able to close down the match. He played two holding midfielders in front of the back four, and he didn't want them getting too far forward.

'Shay, get the ball,' he'd tell his goalkeeper. 'I want you to hit it as far up the pitch as you can.'

It was back to the long ball game. That was all there was to it – the players up front would just have to try to win the ball and create chances. Trap didn't want Shay to ever pass the ball to his own defenders or to the midfielders. He was to hit it long every time.

The new way of playing was a bit hard for Shay to get his head around. He could understand where Trap was coming from, because even if the forwards didn't win the ball, at least it would be away from the danger area. But it did seem a very simplistic strategy which would make it difficult for Ireland to create chances of their own.

Shay played in all ten of the qualifying matches for the 2010 World Cup, delighted to hold on to the number one shirt. Trap's style of play certainly suited the goalkeeper, as it meant fewer goals were conceded. But he did wonder if the fans were missing the excitement of the end to end, high risk games.

Ireland earned some decent draws, but not enough wins for top spot in the group, which went to Italy. If they were to make it to the World Cup in South Africa, Ireland would have to win a playoff once again.

Ireland were drawn against one of the top teams in the playoffs – France. Shay knew it would be a tough task.

The home leg was first, and Ireland put in a pretty poor performance. They were too rigid in their style of play and really didn't look like creating anything. The only goal came from the visitors, with Nicolas Anelka making it 1-0.

Now Ireland had it all to do in the away leg. They'd be playing in the Stade de France, the fantastic stadium just outside Paris.

Trap's instructions to the team were to keep playing the way they had been playing. Keep things tight, don't press too much, just get the ball forward and hope for the best.

The players weren't happy. They didn't think that strategy was going to work, and this was an all or nothing match. If they won they'd be going to the World Cup. If they lost they'd be going nowhere. They had to give it everything they had.

Paris was full of Irish supporters decked out in green. In the days leading up to the match the players saw them everywhere as they were taken to and from training. It gave them a real boost knowing they were so well supported, and they were even more determined to go out there and win it for their fans.

Shay told his teammates exactly what he thought. 'Lads, I don't care what he says, we're going to go at these tonight,' he said. 'We're going to throw everything at them. Whatever happens, if we get beat we get beat – but nobody gets back on this bus without giving it everything. This is the chance of a lifetime. We're going for it.'

The senior players in the team all agreed with him. They had nothing to lose.

Walking out onto the pitch, Shay couldn't believe the number of Irish supporters in the stands. Thousands of them were already singing and waving flags, hoping for a memorable performance from the boys in green.

In the huddle before the game, captain Robbie Keane's message was clear. 'This is why we play, boys, this is where we want to be,' he told them. 'We go out there now and we hit them with everything we've got.'

There was a sense of freedom about the Irish team that night that had been missing for a long time. All over the pitch, they were at the top of their game. Shay had never felt so relaxed playing for Ireland – the knowledge that they had nothing to lose, and everything to gain, was like casting off the shackles.

Half an hour into the game, Robbie Keane blasted the ball into the back of the net. Team and fans alike went crazy. On aggregate, the sides were now level. The World Cup was suddenly within their grasp.

By the end of ninety minutes, Ireland had managed to keep France scoreless. Now they were facing into extra time.

The team huddled together once more. The same air of confidence was clear on everyone's face.

'We've got this!' Robbie told them. 'We can do it.'

Extra time. There was an added edge to the play now, a certain caginess as neither team wanted to concede.

France got a free kick about 25 metres out, and Florent Malouda put a cross into the box. Shay looked for one of his defenders to head it clear, but instead the ball bounced in the box – always a danger.

Thierry Henry was closest to the bounce and he put out his arm to control the ball, first with the inside of his arm, and then with a second touch with his hand.

Shay couldn't believe how blatant Henry's cheating was. He was so close to him he could see the pattern changing on the ball as Henry spun it around, knocking it past Shay with his right leg for William Gallas to get to. Gallas put the ball in the back of the net.

Shay's first thought was that he would take the free kick as quickly as possible, get the ball up the other end and catch the French off guard. He was so sure the referee must have seen the handball that it didn't cross his mind that the goal would stand.

But the referee was pointing at the centre circle.

He was allowing the goal.

Outraged, Shay sprinted over to the referee, banging his arm in the international symbol for 'handball'. 'Handball, handball, ref, handball!' he roared.

As the French fans cheered and waved their flags, Kevin Kilbane rushed over too, backing Shay up. 'He cheated!' he told the referee. 'He handled the ball! You have to have seen it!'

On the sideline, Trapattoni was incandescent with rage, waving his hands in the air and appealing to anyone who would listen.

The referee was paralysed with fear. Shay realised that he couldn't handle ruling the goal out in a stadium full of home fans.

Shay appealed to the linesman, but he was deaf to their pleas. The Irish players looked at each other in shock. It was their worst nightmare. Were they about to be cheated out of the World Cup?

The game restarted. The Irish team were shell shocked, struggling to process what had happened. The Irish fans, not having the benefit of a replay on the big screen, gave it their all in cheering on their team, but a second goal didn't come.

The whistle blew. 1-1 on the night. 2-1 on

aggregate. France were going to the World Cup, and Ireland were going home.

It was the lowest Shay had ever felt in an Irish shirt. Missing out on the 1998 World Cup was bad enough, but at least they knew they had been beaten on merit. To be cheated out of that place was utterly heartbreaking.

Richard Dunne sat on the grass a couple of feet away from Thierry Henry, utterly dejected. Damien Duff wiped away the tears that were flowing down his cheeks.

The team made their way over to their loyal fans, who were still singing in the stands. They clapped them, letting them know how much their support meant to them.

'What did he say to you?' Shay asked Richard as they walked off the pitch. He'd seen him sitting with Henry after the match ended.

'He admitted he handled it,' Richard told him. 'I said it's a bit late for that now!'

'He's lucky he didn't say that to me,' Shay fumed. 'I'd have told him where to go!'

Back in the dressing room, the mood was one of fury. Boots and bags were kicked across the room, drinks flung against the wall.

In the losing dressing rooms Shay had been in before, gloom would settle over the players, a quiet sense of despondency. This time, there was none of that – it was loud, and it was angry.

The players demanded to see a video of the incident. On the replay, Henry's handball was as clear as day.

'How can they get away with that?' Shay raged. 'It's so unfair!'

The team had been working towards the World Cup finals for the last eighteen months, and now their dream had been snatched away.

It was never easy to lose. But playing for your club, there was always another game next week where you could have another go. It would be four years until another World Cup came around.

In the days that followed, the handball was the biggest sports story in the world. It was on the front pages of all the papers. The clip was played again and again on news channels and discussed in homes and workplaces. Would FIFA step in? Was it possible that the match would be replayed?

But Shay knew there was little chance of that.

The referee's decision was always final, it was one of the principles of football that was never ignored.

In his long career on the pitch, nothing would ever hurt as much.

CHAPTER TWENTY-ONE

MOVING ON

Shay knew it was time to find a new club. He wasn't happy to sit on the bench at City any longer. He was getting older now and he was conscious that the clock was ticking down on his career. He needed to make the most of the years he had left. As a sixteen-year-old, he had chosen Celtic over Man United because he believed the Scottish club gave him a better chance of playing. He felt just the same now at the other end of his career.

So he was very pleased when Aston Villa spoke to his agent to express their interest in him.

When he was growing up, Aston Villa had been a big deal, always challenging for the FA Cup, and even for the Premier League in its early seasons.

His Ireland teammate Richard Dunne had already moved to Villa.

Shay took a big pay cut to move to Villa and he knew he was leaving a club that was challenging for titles to go to a club that would be unlikely to do the same. But neither of those things were as important to him now as getting game time.

When he made his debut for Villa against Fulham, it was the first time he'd played in the Premier League in sixteen months. He'd had more game time with Ireland in the last year than he had with City. There was no doubt in his mind that he'd done the right thing. He had a great game, making three fantastic saves. It was the perfect start.

Unfortunately, after that Villa had a tough season. One of the main problems was that they just couldn't seem to turn draws into wins. They were struggling to score goals, and their top scorer only managed nine goals in the whole season.

As the season drew to a close, Villa were in danger of relegation. Shay knew what this would mean to the club – not just the first team and their manager, but everyone connected with it. The kit men, the masseurs, the match day staff – all these people were relying on the success of the team, and they might end up out of work if Villa were relegated.

Shay was desperate to do all he could to keep Villa up. He couldn't score goals, but he could keep them out.

They were into the last seconds of their match against West Brom and it was still scoreless. It had been a tense, edgy match,

West Brom forward Peter Odemwingie was through on goal and the ball fell nicely to him. Shay threw himself in front of the ball, blocking it with his legs. Shay fell back into the net, but, most importantly, the ball stayed out.

Richard Dunne clutched his head with both hands. 'How did you keep that out?'

Shay knew he had saved a vital point for his club. The draw lifted everyone's spirits, and they were able to hold on for the last few matches and avoid the dreaded drop.

CHAPTER TWENTY-TWO

EURO 2012

It was tournament time again. Once again Ireland's route to the finals of the European Championship was through the playoffs.

Shay was delighted when Ireland were drawn against Estonia. He felt it would be easier than some of the other teams they could have faced, and they also had the benefit of playing the second leg at home.

At the away leg in Tallinn, Robbie Keane told the huddle, 'Our fans didn't come all this way to watch us lose. We go at these and we keep going at them until it's done.'

The team took his words to heart. In the end, it was an easy 4-0 win for Ireland. They were as good as through to the finals.

The home match was a much more lacklustre affair, ending in a 1–1 draw. But that didn't matter – what mattered was that they were through! It was wonderful to celebrate in front of their home fans, doing a lap of the stadium.

It had been ten long years since Ireland had played in an international tournament, and Shay was all too aware that this could be his last chance.

When the draw was made for the groups at the tournament, it was clear Ireland's luck had run out. They were drawn against Italy, Spain and Croatia – three of the strongest teams in the finals.

Shay had a tough build-up to the tournament. The team assembled in Ireland for a training camp three weeks before their first match. On the second day, Shay landed awkwardly on his knee and felt something pop.

He knew straight away that something wasn't right.

Shay flew over to the UK to see a knee specialist,

who recommended plenty of rest and ice. Shay took him at his word and started using a compressed ice machine which helped to reduce swelling and pain.

Shay was desperate to recover as quickly as possible and kept using the machine at the highest setting. Unfortunately, he ended up adding to the problem by damaging a nerve on the outside of his knee.

Back in training, he found himself overcompensating for his painful right knee by putting too much weight through his left leg. Before he knew it his left calf was hurting too.

The team flew out to Budapest for a warm-up match against Hungary. Every day, Shay did his training with goalkeeping coach Alan Kelly, and they were careful to protect his injuries. But despite their best efforts he was still having difficulties.

Shay and Alan Kelly went back a long way. They had been roommates on Ireland trips when Alan was still playing, and had always trained together. Shay knew he could trust him completely.

The day before the Hungary match, Alan put Shay through a fitness test. One routine had him hitting twelve shots at Shay as hard as he could –

a mix of volleys, half-volleys, headers and off the ground.

'Good work, Shay,' Alan said. 'How's the knee?'

'It's grand,' Shay said. 'Let's keep going!'

Shay's reflexes felt good and it gave him a boost going into the match. The match went well for him – he made one great reflex save that gave him the confidence that he'd be fine for the Euros.

The team arrived in Poland. As the day of the Croatia match came around, Shay's knee felt better, and he was revved up for the match. After all the build-up to the tournament, the Irish team were dying to get started. With Italy and Spain still to come, they felt they needed to get a win against Croatia to have any hope of making it out of the group.

Unfortunately, the game got off to a bad start. Less than three minutes into the match, Croatia launched their first attack and Mario Mandzukic put a header past Shay. 1-0 Croatia. Shay felt it was a shot he could have saved – he had been wrong-footed and the shot had just drifted past him. It was gutting to concede so early on.

Then Sean St Ledger equalised, and Irish hopes were raised once more. But minutes later, Nikica Jelavic scored to give Croatia the lead, and Ireland went in at halftime 2-1 down.

There was still everything to play for. A one-goal deficit wasn't the end of the world. If they could keep things solid at the back they only needed one decent chance to level things up.

In the second half, Mandzukic scored another header. To add insult to injury, the ball hit the post and bounced off Shay's head before landing in the back of the net. 3-1. The Croatian players wheeled away in joyful celebration, while the Irish lads' shoulders slumped. It was hard to see any way back from here.

After the match, a feeling of despondency settled over the Irish camp. Their hopes had been so high, and now they knew they had a mountain to climb.

Spain were masters of world football, always challenging for titles, always a threat. Even if the Irish team had played at the top of their ability they would have found it tough to overcome them, and on the night they were a long way short of that.

Shay felt that every player, himself included, were just a second late to every ball. Whatever was going wrong, they just couldn't seem to raise their game. In the end, it was an easy 4-0 win for Spain.

After just two games, Ireland were out, their Euro 2012 dreams shattered. The only consolation on the night was the Irish fans. They had started singing Fields of Athenry with ten minutes to go in the game. After the final whistle blew, they stayed where they were, singing it over and over again. The Irish fans were often called the best fans in the world, and it was moments like this that made it so. Where other fans might have shouted abuse at their team after such a big loss, the boys and girls in green had only support for their fallen heroes.

It was a strange feeling having to face into the Italy game knowing they had nothing left to play for but pride. Thousands of Irish fans had already made the trip to Poland for the game, and the team vowed not to let them down.

They played better than they had done in the previous two matches but in the end Italy were too strong for them. Two goals from Antonio Cassano and Mario Balotelli made it 2-0 to Italy.

Ireland were going home. The team felt they had really not done themselves justice in their tournament, devastated to have such a poor record.

Shay knew the time had come to think about his future with Ireland. He was thirty-six now, and although many goalkeepers kept playing into their late thirties or even beyond, it wasn't an easy thing to do. Many players made the decision to give up international football so they could concentrate on their club for the last few years of their careers. It wasn't so much the matches for Ireland that Shay was starting to find hard, but the travel involved and needing to be ready for a club match right after getting home.

He had reached 125 caps, a fantastic achievement and one he could hardly have dreamed of when he started out. And the disappointing performance by the team at Euro 2012 made him feel that maybe it was time to pass on the gloves to someone else.

He spoke to Trapattoni to tell him his decision.

'Shay, I would like you to stay on,' he said. 'But I understand and respect your decision and thank you.'

It was the end of an era, and a sad way to close the door on his international career.

CHAPTER TWENTY-THREE

SECOND CHANCE

Two years later, everything had changed with the Irish football team. Trapattoni was gone, and in his place was Martin O'Neill. His second in command was none other than the former Ireland captain Roy Keane.

Shay found it a bit strange not to be part of it all. A short time after he'd retired, he'd started to have regrets. He rang up Marco Tardelli to say he'd be happy to come back if they wanted him to, but Trap was hesitant. 'I think we need to give the new goalkeepers a chance,' he said.

Shay understood, though it was hard to come to terms with the idea that he'd played for Ireland for the last time.

With the new management team in place, Shay wondered if the door might be open to him coming back. He tried not to get his hopes up too much. He knew he wasn't getting as much game time at Aston Villa as he would have liked.

As well as being assistant manager at the Republic of Ireland, Roy Keane was assistant manager at Villa. Shay liked catching up with his old teammate, and one day after training they were having a coffee together.

'So when are you going to come back to play for Ireland?' Roy asked him out of the blue.

At first Shay just laughed, but Roy had planted a seed in his mind.

A few weeks later, they were playing pool together when Roy brought it up again. 'Why don't you think about it?'

'OK, I will,' Shay said.

Deep down, he was thrilled at the idea of playing for his country again. Roy was keen to encourage him, insisting that he could challenge for the number one jersey, and that his experience would be very valuable to the younger goalkeepers, Keiren Westwood and Darren Randolph.

He told Roy he was open to the idea, and Roy spoke to Martin O'Neill. Martin told Shay he couldn't promise him anything as he wanted to give the new goalies a chance, but he would certainly like to have him as part of the squad.

Shay was happy with that – it was exciting to know the door was open to him coming back.

Meanwhile, he was glad to go out on loan to Middlesbrough, getting some more games in and brushing up on his fitness.

Ahead of a friendly against Oman, Martin O'Neill named his squad. Shay was in it.

He was thrilled to be back in the Ireland camp, though he had to put up with a lot of teasing for returning.

'I thought I'd got rid of you for good!' Robbie said with a grin.

Even though Shay had been gone for two years, he felt part of the group again right away. When he was picked to start against Oman, he was as excited as he had been playing for the very first time. Nothing could beat that feeling of lining up with the boys in green singing the national anthem and getting ready to play for his country.

Shay remained a part of the Republic of Ireland squad. He knew he couldn't expect to start every game anymore, but he was delighted whenever the chance came, and happy to be part of the squad, helping to support the other keepers.

In the meantime, after a spell on loan to Middlesbrough, he left Aston Villa and signed for Stoke. He had really enjoyed his time at Middlesbrough and thought about signing for them, but when the offer came through from Stoke it was too good to refuse, as the location made sense for family reasons. Shayne and Sienna were settled in school in the area, and although he was now divorced from their mother, it meant he could still see them regularly. It was also close to where he was living with his new partner Rebecca, so it meant he wouldn't need to move again.

This time, he knew he'd be joining Stoke as second-choice keeper, but he was resigned to that. He had an important role to play as back-up to Jack Butland and he'd keep pushing for a place.

In October 2015, Ireland faced one of their toughest tests. They were playing Germany, the reigning World Cup holders, in a qualifier for Euro 2016.

During the first half Shay felt an old knee injury flare up. He'd had an operation years earlier and continued wear and tear on the knee was taking its toll. Suddenly his knee became very swollen and stiff. Shay could hardly move. He realised he wasn't going to be able to play on, even to halftime, and he shouted to one of the subs warming up nearby that he needed to come off.

Martin O'Neill made the substitution, sending Darren Randolph on for Shay. Shay was gutted to be stretchered off during such a vital match.

Football was a strange game with many twists of fate. Shay's bad luck turned out to be good luck for Darren, who was making his competitive debut under the most difficult of circumstances. He had a great game. In the second half, he created an assist for Shane Long, who promptly stuck the ball in the back of the German net. 1-0 Ireland! They had beaten the World Champions!

Out injured with his knee, Shay could only watch the rest of the campaign and the playoffs against

Bosnia from his couch, but he was thrilled to see Ireland qualify for Euro 2016. He wondered if he'd be part of the squad who would be chosen to compete. He longed for one last chance at a major tournament.

After an operation on his knee and being out of action for five months, Shay felt his chances of being number one for Stoke or playing again for Ireland were slowly fading away. But then in March 2016 two injuries were to change everything. Stoke keeper Jack Butland broke his ankle playing for England, and Rob Elliot suffered a serious knee injury on duty for Ireland.

Shay would never have wished to benefit from injuries to his teammates, but that was the way football worked. Now he was back into the first team at Stoke, and soon afterwards he found out he had a place in the Ireland squad that was on its way to France for the Euros.

In the friendlies before the tournament, Martin O'Neill tried out both Shay and Darren Randolph, his mind still not made up about who would be his first-choice keeper. Shay felt that Darren had the better chance, but he was fit again and ready to push him hard for that starting place.

In the final pre-tournament match against Belarus, at forty years of age, Shay won his 134th cap for Ireland and became the longest-serving Ireland player of all time. He had represented his country for over twenty years – an outstanding achievement that filled him with huge pride.

CHAPTER TWENTY-FOUR

EURO 2016

When it came to selecting his team, Martin O'Neill was old-fashioned. He only announced the team in the dressing room ninety minutes before kick-off.

With other managers, you could usually guess from the last training session what way they were thinking, with the first eleven lining up for a practice match against the rest of the squad. Under Trapattoni, it had been very clear who he intended to name in his starting team. But with O'Neill, even that last session didn't give the players many clues. They would all have a go at guessing who the chosen team would be, but no one got it right.

So as the team prepared for their opening match

against Sweden, Shay was still hoping he had a chance of being chosen. He remembered the thrill of playing for Ireland at the World Cup in 2002 and at Euro 2012, and prayed for another chance.

But it wasn't to be. When O'Neill read out his team ninety minutes before kick-off, the number one spot went to Darren.

Shay knew he had to overcome his disappointment and get out there and support Darren and the rest of his teammates. His job now was to help Darren warm up and prepare for the match.

For the rest of the tournament, Shay's role was very different from what it had been in 2012. He felt almost like a cheerleader, encouraging the players every step of the way. His experience was a valuable asset to the group, keeping them focused and ready for the task at hand. He knew it was an important job, but it was hard to know that, unless something happened to Darren, he wouldn't be out there on the pitch where he really wanted to be.

After drawing 1-1 with Sweden, Ireland went on to lose 3-0 to Belgium, a result that made Irish spirits sink. Shay tried to cheer his teammates up, reminding them that they still had everything to play for in the last group game against Italy. Martin O'Neill and Roy Keane too were quick to emphasise that the Belgium game was over and done with and they needed to focus on the next one.

No one was happier than Shay when Robbie Brady scored the winner against Italy. In the history of Irish appearances at major tournaments, it was one of the finest wins of all, against a team who had been finalists at Euro 2012.

Tournament hosts France were up next in the knockout game. A fine start from Ireland and a penalty scored by Brady meant Ireland went in at halftime 1-0 up. But French forward Antoine Griezmann scored two second-half goals in quick succession to end Irish dreams.

Their tournament was over, but this time the boys in green felt they had done themselves proud. They saluted their fans, knowing they had played their best and given it all they had.

Shay walked around the stadium with his arm around Robbie Keane, waving an Irish flag and applauding the fans. He and Robbie looked at each other, the sense of something coming to an end shared between them. Both knew they wouldn't be taking part in a major tournament again.

Shay thought back over some of his favourite moments with Ireland. His debut as a nineteen-year-old. Qualifying for the World Cup in that memorable match in Tehran. Playing in Japan and Korea, and the amazing homecoming when tens of thousands of fans had gathered in the Phoenix Park to celebrate the team's achievements. And the crowds who had packed the streets of Lifford to welcome him home, so proud to have seen their local hero play at the World Cup.

Now Shay knew his time with Ireland really had come to an end. The day had come to hang up his goalie gloves, this time for good.

CHAPTER TWENTY-FIVE

COACH SHAY

'Come on, lads! Fast feet!'

The Derby County players were running in and out between cones as first-team coach Shay Given put them through their paces.

'Right, give me five more, then we'll have a five-a-side.'

Shay was loving his new role with Derby County.

After retiring from international duty, Shay's professional career started to wind down. Back at Stoke for the start of the new club season, Shay was first-choice keeper. Jack Butland was still out injured and although Shay had fierce competition from Lee Grant, he was the one who the manager opted to keep.

But after a few bad results, Shay found himself dropped from the team, and knew that his time at the club would soon be coming to an end. He began to look to the future. What would life look like after football? Although he'd enjoyed doing media work, providing analysis on matches for Ireland when he was out injured, he preferred a life closer to the pitch. He began taking his UEFA coaching badges, hoping to move on to a new stage of his career. Family life, too, was full and happy. Shay and Rebecca now had two little girls, Gracie and Cassie, who kept them very busy.

In 2018 he was appointed goalkeeping coach at Derby County under manager Frank Lampard. In their playing days, Frank had scored plenty of goals against Shay, as a talented midfielder for Chelsea. Now they'd be working together, bringing their different skills to a new team.

Shay loved the job, working closely with three or four goalkeepers. At first it was strange being the one leading the drills instead of taking part as a player. But he was keen to share all he had learned in his twenty-five years' experience as a goalie with a new generation.

Then came an even bigger role. After Wayne Rooney was appointed manager of the club in January 2021, he made Shay his first-team coach. Like Frank Lampard, Wayne had caused Shay plenty of heartache in the past! He was the record goal scorer for both Man United and England. Now they were on the same side, and they were on a mission to save Derby together.

The new job meant Shay would be working with the whole team, and he relished the opportunity. It was a whole new challenge working with outfield players, putting them through their drills, showing them where they needed to be on the pitch, and helping the manager with his team selection.

One of his players was the young Ireland international Jason Knight. Watching Jason train made him think back to his own early days with Celtic, and all the hopes and dreams of a young player just starting out on a club and international career.

Standing at the side of the pitch, helping his team prepare for their Saturday game, Shay thought how lucky he was to still be involved in the game he had loved all his life. From his long career between the posts to the vital spot on the sideline, Shay could never have enough. He loved the game of football just as much as he had all those years ago when he was a young boy growing up in Donegal, throwing himself down in the mud of his front garden to block shots from the boots of his big brothers.

SHAY GIVEN'S ACHIEVEMENTS

International

Longest-serving Republic of Ireland footballer – twenty years, 1996–2016

134 caps

World Cup Finals 2002

European Championship 2012

European Championship 2016

Nations Cup winners 2011

Club

FA Cup winner's medal 2010–11 (Manchester City)

FA Cup runner-up medal 2014–15 (Aston Villa)
FA Cup runner-up medal 1997–98 (Newcastle)

Individual Honours

FAI Senior International Player of the Year 2005, 2006
Newcastle United FC Player of the Year 2005–06
PFA Team of the Year 2001–02 Premier League, 2005–06 Premier League

ACKNOWLEDGEMENTS

Thank you to Shay Given for kindly agreeing to my telling his story, and for so many amazing memories cheering on the boys in green. Thank you to my husband Aidan Fitzmaurice for reading one draft after another without complaint, for giving me lots of helpful ideas and for answering my many queries about football. Thank you to Neil O'Riordan for sharing his article, which gave a wonderful insight into the schoolboy footballer Shay. Thank you to Rachel and Sarah for their endless support and encouragement. Thank you to my wonderful editor Helen Carr who is always a joy to work with. Thank you to Prin Okonkwo for her eagle-eyed fact checking – much appreciated. Any mistakes that remain are my own. And thank you to the rest of the fantastic team at the O'Brien Press.